When the Preacher
CAME TO
TOWN

By Emma Cane

A Promise at Bluebell Hill
The Cowboy of Valentine Valley
True Love at Silver Creek Ranch
A Town Called Valentine

Novellas
When the Rancher Came to Town
A Wedding in Valentine
The Christmas Cabin
(from the All I Want for Christmas Is a Cowboy anthology)

When the Rancher
CAME TO
TOWN

A VALENTINE VALLEY NOVELLA

EMMA CANE

AVONIMPULSE
An Imprint of HarperCollinsPublishers

Excerpt from *Sleigh Bells in Valentine Valley* copyright © 2014 by Gayle Kloecker Callen.

Excerpt from *The Cowboy and the Angel* copyright © 2014 by Tina Klinesmith.

Excerpt from *Finding Miss McFarland* copyright © 2014 by Vivienne Lorret.

Excerpt from *Take the Key and Lock Her Up* copyright © 2014 by Lena Diaz.

Excerpt from *Dylan's Redemption* copyright © 2014 by Jennifer Ryan.

Excerpt from *Sinful Rewards 1* copyright © 2014 by Cynthia Sax.

Excerpt from *Whatever It Takes* copyright © 2014 by Dixie Brown.

Excerpt from *Hard to Hold On To* copyright © 2014 by Laura Kaye.

Excerpt from *Kiss Me, Captain* copyright © 2014 by Gwen T. Weerheim-Jones.

EPub Edition SEPTEMBER 2014 ISBN: 9780062369529
Print Edition ISBN: 9780062369536

10 9 8 7 6 5 4 3 2 1

To Jen Suarez and Missy Gerstan: You started out as neighbors, and now you've become dear friends. Thanks so much for cooking challenges, movie dates, the peaceful garden view, nail polish artistry, and fun evenings on the back porch or around the fire!

Chapter 1

Mason Lopez pulled his pickup into a parking spot next to Connections Bed and Breakfast in Valentine Valley, Colorado. Though only a couple blocks off Main Street, the B&B looked remote, surrounded by trees and lush summer gardens. Not that he was going to enjoy it all that much. He had a business meeting at the Sweetheart Ranch that started in an hour. He'd arrived early to check in, hoping it wouldn't inconvenience the innkeeper too much. Maybe he should have called. Getting out of his pickup, he could smell the earthy moisture of Silver Creek, which ran behind the B&B, a rambling old Victorian gem of a building. It had three stories, painted yellow, with white trim around all the windows and the wraparound porches. White wicker furniture and potted plants made the porches seem like an oasis of calm, and multicolored impatiens hung from baskets centered between the porch posts. He'd read on the website that the place was the first home built in Valentine that wasn't a miner's shack, back in the early 1880s. Someone had treated it with loving care, restoring it for guests to enjoy.

He'd been to Valentine before, but never overnight. His family owned the Lake Ridge Ranch and Cattle Company up in the mountains near the small town of Elk's Crest. It was only about a half hour drive from Valentine, but since there were meetings today and tomorrow, there was no point in driving back and forth.

He grimaced. And there was the Silver Creek Rodeo on Saturday. He'd signed up to compete, and he wasn't exactly looking forward to it. It had been five years since he'd been on the professional bull riders' tour. He'd had to retire due to an injury and his dad's bout with cancer, but he hoped that competing again would get the attention of Nate Thalberg of the Silver Creek Ranch. Mason's ranch and stock contracting business was on the man's list as a possible investment, but Nate had warned him up front that he took his time researching and making a fair decision. Mason no longer had time to wait. His dad had made a few shaky business decisions when he'd been ill, and now a loan repayment had come due, surprising them all, including his embarrassed father.

Mason swung his bag out of the backseat and jogged up the steps. He'd never stayed in a B&B, preferring dive motels early in his rodeo career or his RV later on, now long since sold. A B&B had just seemed girly. But he'd been lucky to get a room at all on rodeo weekend.

Once inside, the scent of something baking wafted around him, and he inhaled deeply of cinnamon and other spices as he took off his Stetson. Connections wasn't all that girly, though there were lace curtains in the windows. He was standing in a front entrance hall, with a wide staircase leading up to the next floor. Overhead, mahogany beams intersected in a square pattern. Carved wooden columns separated the hall from the long parlor, which seemed to run to the back of the house. The lower walls were paneled, and the upper had striped wallpaper. He noticed polished antiques: a display cabinet with a selection of glass vases; wingback chairs intermixed with fancy little tables, some of them glass- or marble-topped; the rolling, curved backs of old-fashioned couches upholstered in yellow or maroon velvet.

On the other side of the hall, curtained French doors were ajar, letting him glimpse bookshelves lining one wall. He could hear women's voices from inside, a mixture of elderly ladies and one younger woman with a voice that was rather deep and sexy. The women weren't being quiet. Mason circled his hat in his hands and felt like an eavesdropper, but he had to check in and change into fresh clothes for his meeting. Maybe they'd finish up soon . . .

"Look," said the younger woman with a touch of polite exasperation, "I know it was rude of me to ignore your later e-mails, but I did answer the first one—and my answer was no. I'm happy Valentine Valley is trying a new Wild West Weekend for the tourists to go along with the rodeo, but Connections doesn't need to be a part of it. We're off the beaten path—they won't want to walk away from Main Street just to see a B&B. And the event starts in two days—isn't it a little late to worry about convincing me, when you ladies obviously have so much to do?"

"Amanda, they will want to see a buildin' that's so important to women's history," said an old lady with a strong Western accent.

"Mrs. Palmer—"

"No, no, hear me out. This lovely house was goin' to be torn down willy nilly, as if it hadn't once been used as a brothel with poor Chinese immigrant ladies."

Mason's eyes widened, and he couldn't help glancing around, intrigued. A brothel, huh?

Amanda said, "I know that if it hadn't been for you ladies, it *would* have been torn down, and I can't thank you enough for saving Connections for me to eventually own."

"You did hear the story about what we were forced to do," said another elderly woman, her voice melodious and good-natured.

"Some of it, of course, Mrs. Thalberg. It's a legend around here, even for people like me, who haven't been in town all that long."

Mrs. Thalberg chuckled. "I can still see Connie setting aside her walker and putting manacles on her wrists."

Mrs. Palmer's laugh was a cackle of delight. "The mayor tried to stop us from chainin' ourselves to the front porch, but he didn't dare put his hands on us."

A third woman said with the voice of a proper schoolteacher, "It was necessary to show we would not be deterred. I did not mind the manacles. And we were successful. We will not hesitate to employ the same tactics with you, young lady."

Mason barely stopped a snort of laughter.

"Are you going to chain yourself to my front porch until I give in, Mrs. Ludlow?" Amanda asked, her voice laced with reluctant amusement.

"Most likely not," Mrs. Ludlow replied coolly. "But I simply don't understand why you wish to abstain. We have ample nineteenth-century costumes for you to choose from."

And for a moment, Mason wondered how the young woman with the sexy voice would look dressed scandalously . . .

Amanda seemed to be thinking along the same lines. "You can't expect I'd want to costume myself like a resident of a brothel."

"No, no, of course not," Mrs. Thalberg assured her. "As the owner, you'd be the madam."

Mason heard a choked cough, probably from Amanda, and it made him grin.

"Next thing you'll want my guests to be prostitutes."

"Well, only if they want to," Mrs. Ludlow said matter-of-factly. "Saloon girls would be the better choice. We've already put together a brochure of the town history where Connections is mentioned. It will be wonderful for tourism—and for your prospective guests, of course. There's a bit more involved, but we'll be discussing it all in detail at the meeting tonight at the community center. We think you should attend."

"I know my B&B has some important history," Amanda said, "but don't you think it's a little . . . icky to dramatize the poor women who were forced into prostitution, for what's supposed to be a fun family event?"

"Surely you know your home's history," Mrs. Ludlow said. "The next owner was a con woman, who specialized in luring men into her house and getting them inebriated enough to think they'd enjoyed the favors of the young saloon girls, when in reality she was fleecing them of their money. This 'madam' even had a dalliance with the local sheriff, who made sure the men caused no trouble. Surely you see how play-acting this could be amusing."

There was a weighted silence that the elderly women did not break. Mason imagined them staring Amanda down. He had to wonder why she didn't just say she'd go to the meeting. Then the ladies couldn't say she hadn't given them a fair hearing.

And then he realized it was none of his business, that he was letting a low, sexy voice draw him in.

"Ladies, I can only promise to think about it," Amanda said firmly.

He heard a rustle of movement and hoped she was drawing this meeting to a close, so he could check in.

"But now I really have to get back to work. I have a guest arriving in an hour and—"

The French doors both opened wide, and Mason put on a polite smile. The gaggle of ladies came to such an abrupt stop that the back two bumped into the front two. The walker just missed his shin.

"Ladies, I'm Mason Lopez, and I'm early for check-in."

If Amanda was at all annoyed, it only showed with a brief narrowing of her deep blue eyes, maybe because he hadn't announced himself right away. And perhaps he should have.

Her smile was gracious as she extended a hand. "Mr. Lopez, I'm Amanda Cramer, the owner of Connections."

Her grip was warm and firm. "You can call me Mason."

She was a tall woman, with the kind of generous curves that made a man want to see what was beneath her jeans and sleeveless V-necked shirt. Her sandy blond hair was gathered back in a ponytail, emphasizing high cheekbones and severe brows, her skin pale, as if she never saw the sun. This was a no-nonsense businesswoman if he ever saw one. He couldn't imagine her dressing up as a brothel madam, even for these old ladies.

"Well, well," said one elderly woman, eyeing him up and down like he was her favorite apple pie. "I'm Mrs. Palmer. You must be here for the rodeo."

The Western drawl belonged to the woman wearing a big blond wig with a bow in it, lots of makeup, and a dress with a wild pattern of linked horseshoes. He wasn't sure he'd ever seen anything like it. Must be in honor of the Wild West Weekend.

"Yep, I'm competing in the bull riding," he answered, trying to keep his ambivalence hidden. "I have some business in town, too."

"Mr. Lopez, my name is Mrs. Ludlow," said the woman with the schoolteacher voice. "Where are you from, young man?"

Of the three of them, she was the only one who looked like the typical grandma, with pressed slacks and a white blouse, wearing a sweater over her shoulders although it was an unusually warm day for summer in the Rockies. It was her walker that had almost collided with his shins.

"My ranch is near Elk's Crest, ma'am," he said, nodding to her.

"I'm Mrs. Thalberg," said the third elderly lady. "Which ranch do you mean?"

She had curly red hair, and her makeup was subtle and flattering. She wore jeans and a vest over a top, and her good-natured smile matched her voice.

"Not just being nosy for no reason," she explained before he could answer. "My family owns the Silver Creek Ranch."

Of course—Nate must be her grandson. "I'm with the Lake Ridge Ranch and Cattle Company, ma'am. We're providing some of the rough stock for the rodeo."

"Oh, Lake Ridge. I think my late husband knew your granddad."

Mason grinned. "Probably. My *abuelo* knew everyone."

During this exchange, Amanda kept a smile in place, looking both gracious and interested, but he got the faintest feeling that she was very good at putting on a mask. But then, she was in the hospitality business. It wouldn't look good to be bored by a guest.

"You'll love stayin' here," Mrs. Palmer said in a confidential voice, her hand on his arm. "Amanda knows how to take care of people. Remind her to come to the rodeo."

Amanda sighed and shook her head. "I don't think so, Mrs. Palmer. It's a busy weekend for me."

All three ladies gave her pointed looks. If Mason had been a kid, he'd have jumped to attention and agreed to anything to avoid those well-intentioned looks.

Mrs. Ludlow glanced at him. "Young man, if you can't

get her to attend the rodeo, then remind her about tonight's meeting. I'm certain that, standing here in the hall, you heard all about it."

Caught in the act of eavesdropping, he couldn't deny it, so he only said, "I'll do what I can, ma'am." Amanda was frowning, so he hastened to add, "But I'm a stranger, so I wouldn't blame Ms. Cramer for taking my advice lightly."

"Now that would be a mistake," Mrs. Palmer said, "ignorin' a fine cowboy like yourself."

Mason glanced at Amanda, feeling a little desperate.

"Ladies, why don't you let the poor man check in," Amanda said. "It sounds like you'll see him this weekend."

"I hope before that," Mrs. Palmer said with a wink.

Was she flirting with him? He gave her his best rodeo-tour smile—cheerful but devoid of real depth, the one he'd used when he hadn't wanted to give any encouragement to the buckle bunnies who followed the rodeo tour. He wasn't sure if anyone had ever called an elderly woman a buckle bunny . . .

"Come join us tonight, Amanda," Mrs. Thalberg encouraged as the ladies moved to the door in a cluster.

Mason opened the door for them.

"She already said she'd think about it, Rosemary," Mrs. Ludlow said. "No need to browbeat the girl. Good day, Mr. Lopez."

Mason closed the door behind them and caught Amanda sizing him up. She didn't blush.

"I apologize for forgetting to call and let you know I'd be arriving early," Mason said.

"It's okay. You're just lucky they were here"—she gestured to the front door—"or otherwise I could have been gone, leaving you unable to check in at all."

"Then it's a good thing for me. Need to change out of my travel clothes."

She was still studying him, and he let it happen without comment. It wasn't an interested sort of look, to his regret. He would be a guest in her home, and he'd already disobeyed a rule, it seemed, so she was evaluating him.

"So this Wild West Weekend sounds fun," he finally said.

She arched a brow.

"But a lot of work for you," he quickly added, "especially at the last minute."

"I won't be doing it, so it doesn't matter to me."

"What, you can't picture me and your other guests draped over a porch railing luring in customers?"

He wanted to hear her laugh, but all she did was wince.

"The other guests are members of a female country group, the Sassafras Girls," she explained. "I didn't tell the widows, because I didn't want to give them ideas."

"The widows?"

"That's what we call them. The three old ladies live in the Widows' Boardinghouse across the creek from me. And no, they don't take in boarders. They just like the name. They even have a sign out front labeled with it, but they're on Silver Creek Ranch land, so it's not like tourists see it as an advertisement for a place to stay."

"They seem . . . busy."

She chuckled, and he was glad she was beginning to thaw.

"*Busy* isn't even enough of a word for them. They're the main committee members of the Valentine Valley Preservation Fund. Everything they do is to support the town, encouraging small businesses and helping with historic renovations. From what the previous owner told me, they were instrumental in getting him a grant to remodel and create Connections."

He looked around. "They did a great job. And it's obvious you keep it up real well."

"Thank you. Now why don't you come into the library and you can check over the paperwork you filled out online. I'll need a form of identification and your credit card, please."

She was swift and competent with the check-in, then gave him a quick tour of the public rooms, including the dining room beyond the library, where drinks were available along with a bottomless cookie jar. She pointed through the French doors of the dining room to an expansive garden, complete with wandering paths, fountains, and a gazebo-enclosed hot tub, all of which she assured him he was welcome to use.

At a brief flash of gray fur across the hall, he arched a brow at her, and she smiled.

"My cat, Blue," she explained. "He's very respectful of closed doors. I did mention it on the website, in case of allergies . . ."

"No allergies, so no worries."

They continued the tour, and he found himself studying Amanda Cramer more than the surroundings, asking himself why he was so curious about her. Her participation in the Wild West Weekend was her private business—maybe it was the fact that she intended to skip the rodeo. He hated to think she worked so hard that she didn't enjoy life.

Of course, who was he to talk? Lately, it was hard to find a Saturday evening to hang out at the local bar.

At last he picked up his bag and followed Amanda up the carpeted stairs. He did his best to disguise the fact that he was checking her out from behind. She glanced over her shoulder at him, and he swiftly met her eyes.

"I thought I'd put you in Castle Peak, the only suite on the third floor. That way, if the Sassafras Girls get a little rowdy, at least it won't be over your head."

"I'll try not to be too rowdy over their heads," he teased.

She didn't turn around, only continued up to the next floor.

"Castle Peak?" he said. "Named after the mountain?"

"All four suites are named after the fourteeners of the Elk Mountains—the ones at or above fourteen thousand feet. The others are Snowmass Peak, Pyramid Peak, and Capitol Peak."

"Nice idea."

"Thanks. It's better than Suite number one, number two . . ."

She opened a door on the third floor to a light, airy room, white curtains billowing from the breeze through the open windows. The ceiling with exposed beams sloped up to the top of the house, but it was high enough that he wouldn't hit his head. A large old-fashioned white-iron bed was directly beneath a skylight, bookended on each side by tables with those stacked-globe lamps that made him think of the old west. A curved rocking chair rested before the gas fireplace. The marble-topped bureau was adorned with fresh flowers. Old-west accents decorated the room: a spittoon in the corner, a pitcher and basin on another table, framed black-and-white daguerreotypes on the walls. Through a door, he could see the clawfoot tub in the otherwise sleek and modern bathroom.

"You've done a nice job decorating everything in the house," he said.

She smiled, and now that they were no longer talking about the rodeo or the Wild West Weekend, she seemed more relaxed, happier. She obviously loved her work. It softened the angles of her face, brought a sparkle to her deep blue eyes that had been missing.

"Thanks," she said. "I admit I spend way too much time on eBay and craigslist, hunting down furniture and knickknacks."

"And there're a lot of antique stores up and down the Roaring Fork Valley."

She gave the briefest hesitation before saying, "Yes, you're right, and those are fun, too."

She handed over a set of keys and became an innkeeper again, explaining the binder on the desk, where she'd listed the Wi-Fi password, restaurants, maps, local sightseeing, and a schedule of events in Valentine that weekend. She pointed out her cell phone number on the key chain.

"I live here, but I can't guarantee I'm around during the day, so you can always reach my cell phone. The other tag is the keypad combination for the front door, in case it's locked. I'll freshen up the room during the day while you're gone, but I only change the sheets every three days, unless you request it."

"No, that's fine." He was starting to wonder what time it was, but didn't want to offend her by glancing at his watch.

"In the evening, there's always a snack in the parlor or the dining room, so you're welcome to help yourself if I'm not around. I serve a hot breakfast, but I need to know roughly when you'll be down."

"Is eight all right? I have a nine o'clock meeting."

"That's fine. Knock on the kitchen door if I don't hear you, but since these floors are old and creaky, I can usually tell when someone's coming down to eat."

"I'll keep that in mind if I decide to explore the house."

She grinned. "You're welcome to. Now I'll leave you in peace to get to your meeting. If you need something, give me a call. Enjoy your weekend at Connections."

She closed the door behind her, and he heard the quiet squeak of the floorboards as she started down the stairs. At last he looked at his watch—and grimaced. Good thing Valentine Valley wasn't a large town. He just hoped he wouldn't be late for his meeting at the Sweetheart Ranch.

But even as he took a quick shower and threw on a clean pair of jeans and Western shirt, he thought of Amanda, and why she was so against helping out the widows for a good cause. She seemed like a nice person—but he knew all about showing the world only what you wanted everyone to see.

Chapter 2

Two hours later, Amanda was baking a peach pie for that evening's snack under the sleepy, watchful eyes of Blue, when she heard the front door open and close. Since the rest of her guests weren't arriving until tomorrow, she knew it had to be Mason Lopez.

His march up the main staircase didn't have the quickness he'd shown on the way down; in fact, he sounded almost slow and ponderous—certainly not the tread of a handsome, fit cowboy.

Okay, so he is handsome, she told herself, pushing a little harder on the rolling pin as she rolled out the dough. He had dark good looks, and his hair was short and shiny, with a little curl to it. His eyes were just as black as his hair, thick-fringed enough that even she was envious. He had the straight, strong nose and cheekbones an art class would want to draw.

With those broad shoulders and muscular thighs en-

cased in jeans, he looked like the other cowboys she occasionally saw striding along Main Street. There were
plenty of small operations scattered between Aspen and
Glenwood Springs. Mason's ranch wasn't in the valley but
farther up into the Elk Mountains, south of Carbondale.
Okay, so she'd been curious and had looked it up. Now she
understood the "and Cattle Company" part of his family
business. They provided horses, cattle, and bulls for rodeos.
She wondered if that was why he was in town—that, along
with entering the rodeo himself. She couldn't help wincing
at the thought of submitting yourself to that much point-
less danger just to entertain a crowd of strangers.

The thought of being there made her shiver with unease,
and she returned to her contemplation of her new guest.
She was getting good at that, telling herself whenever she
felt nervous, to just think of something less stressful.

Apparently Mason Lopez didn't quite have the good
manners of a typical cowboy, because he'd stood in her
front hall and eavesdropped. She let the crust drop into
the glass pie plate, wishing it made a loud, satisfying
thwack to show her annoyance. To be fair, he'd probably
thought he was being polite, waiting his turn. She just
didn't like knowing someone had overheard her denying
the widows something that would help the community.
She was even upset with herself at the speed of her refusal,
knowing how hard she'd been working lately to step out of
her comfort zone, to take chances in a public setting.

Reaching for the bowl of peach slices, she thought
about why, deep in her gut, she was so against exposing
herself to random groups of strangers walking in the door

all weekend. She housed strangers on a regular basis and enjoyed it.

She'd been a lawyer, although she no longer practiced since buying the B&B. Talking to people had always come naturally—until her friendliness had put her in the kind of danger that had cost her her self-confidence and her belief in the decency of people.

Everyone had always told her that the residents of Washington, D.C., were ruthless, but when she'd lived there, she'd never believed it. The government had been her goal through college and law school; a summer internship with her senator had led to a job in his office upon graduation. She'd thought all her dreams had come true, that she'd been respected and had proven her skills both in court and in the senator's office.

And then it had all crashed down around her. She'd only lasted another year in Washington, feeling like an infamous outcast, whispered about wherever she'd gone. Oh, some of that whispering had been by supporters, some by enemies, but in the end, it had all felt the same. The worst had been good friends who'd turned against her. Sick at heart, she'd fled back to her parents' home in Denver. For a year she'd worked in a small firm there, going by her middle name, Amanda, rather than Lauren, but she'd found that even after several years in Denver, people had still known who she was.

She'd quit work with enough in the bank to last her a half dozen years if she was careful. She'd gone to Aspen to do some skiing, though she'd hated the thought of hotels where people might recognize her again. Instead, she'd discovered the calm, simple world of bed-and-breakfasts, the feeling of privacy and personal care they gave. She'd spent a month at a B&B, then the owner had asked her to manage the place for the weekend so that she could tend her sick mother. Amanda had discovered a love of nurturing and nesting she hadn't imagined existed beneath her cynical lawyer persona, and her hunt for her own B&B had started soon after. It had taken months of exploring the Rockies before she'd found Connections up for sale. Valentine Valley had been everything she'd wanted: small and quiet, with peaceful neighbors who—mostly—minded their own business. She'd lived here for a year now, still infatuated with her historic home, focused on growing her business.

She met new people every day; she couldn't be called a hermit, like her mom had accidentally let slip. Not even insulted, Amanda had laughed, but she hadn't realized until later the truth in her mother's innocent words. At the time, she'd told herself that not having a best friend or a boyfriend didn't make her a hermit. After all, not only her enemies had turned on her; so had her supposed friends. It was hard to trust people again.

But those had all been excuses.

With the pie in the oven, Amanda set the timer on her phone, changed into old clothes suitable for gardening, smeared on sunscreen, and headed outside. The grounds of the B&B took just as much work as the inside. She'd hired a landscaper for some of the major stuff like lawn and tree care, but the flowers, shrubs and design work were all hers. She felt at peace in her garden, with the high bushes that formed walls on either side. The terraced lawn sloped down amidst rock gardens to Silver Creek, where she kept kayaks, canoes, and paddleboards for her guests. She had little hidden walkways between tall shrubs, where unusual fountains greeted guests as a reward for their curiosity. She'd strung lights between the trees, and at night, her garden was like her own private fairy world.

One she had to share with guests, of course.

As she headed across the deck, which was partially covered by an arbor, she glanced toward the hot tub beneath the gazebo and did a double take. Mason Lopez sat alone on the edge of the hot tub, his jeans rolled up to his knees, his feet immersed. Though he stared at the bubbling water, he seemed to be looking inward.

She must have made a sound, because he suddenly turned his head. For a moment, she felt pinned by his gaze, aware of him as a man in a way she hadn't felt about anyone in a long time.

She shook it off and said, "Sorry to disturb you." She was about to leave him in peace but found herself saying instead, "Is everything all right?"

He smiled, white teeth gleaming out of the shadows of the gazebo, but it was a tired smile that quickly died.

"Sure, everything's fine. My meeting just didn't go as expected."

She felt frozen, unable to just leave him when he'd said something so personal. "I bet you'll be able to work it out."

A corner of his mouth quirked up. "I'm glad you're sure of that."

"You're not?" Where had that come from? And then

she walked toward him, when she should have been giving him his privacy. But he looked so alone.

"Will you join me?" he asked.

She was surprised to hear a thread of hope in his voice. As a person who *enjoyed* being alone, this felt foreign to her, but the need to help a guest overruled that. She sat down cross-legged beside him. They didn't talk at first, and she watched him rub his shoulder.

He noticed her stare and gave a chagrined smile. "I injured it years ago. It still occasionally aches."

"I imagine the hard work of ranching contributes to that."

"Yeah, it does, but it's worth it. I love working the land that's been in my family for almost seventy-five years. But we've been going through a tough time, and it's been pretty obvious we need a championship bull to invigorate our breeding program. I thought if I met with some of the ranchers here, we could find some investment partners."

"That was what your meeting was about today?"

"Yeah. But the Sweetheart Ranch is a large operation, and it's all they want to handle right now."

"We have other ranches around here."

He glanced at her and grinned. "Yeah, I have more meetings tomorrow."

"I'm sure you'll be successful." She looked away from him, the magnetism of his smile making her feel over-heated though she was sitting in the shade. Or maybe it was the proximity to the hot tub, she told herself. "Is Lake Ridge Ranch a large operation?"

"Not really. There's me and two of my four sisters—"

"Four sisters! I'm an only child—I can't imagine so

much togetherness. Are you the oldest, youngest, or in the middle?"

"I'm the baby of the family."

She gave an exaggerated wince. "The apple of your mom's eye, I bet."

"I might have gotten my way now and again," he agreed with a wink.

They shared a smile that felt companionable and easy, something she didn't normally feel with people right away.

She cleared her throat and looked down at her fingers twisted in her lap. "So you and your sisters work the ranch?"

"And my dad, and an uncle who's a part-time hand. Mom takes care of the house and the fruit and vegetable gardens. But my dad . . ."

He trailed off, and now she noticed the strain in his furrowed brow, the tension in his shoulders. She waited patiently.

"He was sick a few years back and made some decisions without telling the rest of us. He regrets it now, of course, but it put us in a shaky financial condition."

"I'm so sorry, Mason. That's got to be tough for your dad and all of you." She understood pride and worry for a family business, and a pang of sympathy made her put her hand on his forearm.

He nodded his gratitude but didn't speak, and she didn't move her hand. They sat there for several minutes, listening to the piercing whistle of chickadees calling to each other, the breeze bringing the moist, earthy scent of the creek.

"I hope sitting out here eases your thoughts," she said in a soft voice. "I'm sure you'll make it work out—you seem to be pretty driven. Is the rodeo your reward for working so hard?"

The tension seemed to ease out of him as he leaned back, bracing himself with his arms, palms on the deck. "I'm hoping that if I do well, I can get a certain rancher to notice me."

"That might work," she said, eyeing him with amusement. It must be difficult for people *not* to notice him, big and handsome as he was. "Of course, you'd probably have to win."

"I always win," he said with good-natured arrogance.

They were smiling into each other's eyes, and she was suddenly intimately aware that they were alone. Her smile faded and her breathing grew shallow.

His gaze dropped to her mouth. "You're a very good listener," he said, his voice gone husky.

She was about to say *It comes with the business,* but she didn't want to break this spell that wove around them. "Thanks."

But this *was* her business. As the owner, she had to be professional. She looked away from him but restrained herself from jumping so swiftly to her feet that it would seem rude.

"Well, I should get back to my gardening," she said.

"Of course. You must be very busy, keeping this place up yourself."

"Well, I do enjoy it, but I have an assistant innkeeper who helps me with the cooking and cleaning. Sometimes the garden can be put off, but I have some free time today, since the other guests won't start arriving until tomorrow."

"So does that mean you'll have time to attend the Wild West Weekend meeting tonight?"

She lifted one brow. "So you're doing the bidding of the widows after all?"

He raised both hands and smiled. "No pressure, sorry. Though they're definitely an intimidating force, I wouldn't use the same tactics on you. I'm just curious why you're not interested."

She made a face, resting one elbow on her knee and her chin on her fist. "It's awfully last minute." She felt uncomfortable being put on the spot, but she couldn't imagine telling him the truth. That was her business, not his. And then he seemed to realize the same thing.

"I don't mean to intrude. I guess it's just . . . I spend a lot of my time trying to think of creative ways to advertise our stock contracting business. I just thought it was a simple way for you to advertise Connections, especially with its notorious past. I mean—the widows chained themselves to your front porch!"

She gave a reluctant laugh. "I thought for sure you were going to mention the nineteenth-century prostitutes."

"Well, that's fascinating enough, but imagine how many people live in Valentine and know the widows."

"My understanding is that that's everybody," she said ruefully.

"Heck, the whole town might even have watched the festivities as the old ladies stopped a construction crew."

"Oh, you're so sure it went that far?"

He chuckled. "No, but I have a vivid imagination. The details don't matter. But I bet there are a lot of locals who've never seen what this place was transformed into and are really curious. And that would lead to recommendations to their families and friends, right?"

"You are way too logical."

"And brilliant, I know, but you still sound reluctant. Will it be that much work?"

"I . . . I don't know."

"And maybe it's not the extra work?" he asked, eyeing her curiously.

She looked away, swallowing hard. After the scandal that had destroyed her law career in politics, she'd lived with the feeling of anxiety for years, until she'd fled to the world of B&Bs and discovered a new kind of peace—but a temporary one. The widows only wanted her to have fun, and it bothered her that she was still so reluctant.

"You're right, I should at least hear the whole plan," she finally said.

"It sounds like fun," he said. "And those widows are a riot. Mind if I go?"

She gazed at him curiously. "I don't think you'll meet many ranchers there."

"I know, but I don't have any plans, and maybe we can get a drink afterward."

He was asking her out! It had been so long that she almost didn't recognize the signs. But there had been that moment where she'd thought about kissing him, and she was pretty certain he'd been thinking about it, too. She felt as fluttery as a high school girl before her first prom. It had been *way* too long.

"I—maybe," she said. "I guess it depends on how long the meeting lasts."

"Fair enough."

"And I made a pie for your evening snack and—" She gasped and pulled her phone out of her pocket. Whew, the timer said she had a few minutes to spare. "I better get it out of the oven before it burns."

"We can't have that. What time do you want me to meet you in the front hall tonight?"

Part of her wanted to decline, and part of her was desperate for a man's flattering attention. "Uh . . . we can walk. It's only a block away. Is quarter of seven okay?"

"Sure, gives me time to get a quick bite to eat."

She prayed he wouldn't ask her out for dinner, too, and when he didn't, she was relieved. Mostly.

"If you don't want to traipse all the way back to your room to look at your binder, I can recommend the Silver Creek Café. It's just a block east of here."

"Great, thanks. See you this evening."

He grabbed a towel she kept stacked in an alcove. As she hurried away, he began drying off his feet.

Oh my God, she had a date. She should be excited—and she was, she thought, opening the screen door that led to the kitchen. But she was nervous, too, a feeling that cramped her stomach uncomfortably. She didn't like being nervous; she had spent too many years feeling that way. It was just a drink.

And a meeting with lots of people who would try to persuade her to participate in a town event. But it was time for her to take these next steps in her recovery.

Chapter 3

MASON ATE OUT on the deck of the Silver Creek Café, surrounded by an abundance of potted ferns and flowers, with greenery laced in an arbor overhead. The occasional kayaker paddled by down the creek. Drinking a cup of coffee at the end of the meal, he found himself remembering his talk with Amanda.

He couldn't believe he'd opened up about his dad's situation, something he never usually did. It was a family matter, and there was no need to bring other people down. But she'd been a compassionate listener, and he'd found himself confiding in her in a way that wasn't possible with his sisters or mother. Amanda had sympathized, without making him feel awkward or regretful.

Then his thoughts focused more on her, and the kiss that had almost happened. It had seemed to shimmer in the air between them, a promise of pleasure. He'd like to try that again, this time culminating in an actual kiss.

But first they would attend the committee meeting together. He wasn't sure what had made him propose it, except that something about her reaction to the Wild West Weekend bothered him. And just now, he'd discovered another piece to the puzzle that was Amanda. When he'd told the server at the café about Amanda's referring him there, the server had been surprised, saying they'd all seen her from a distance, working in her garden, but she'd never come in for a meal.

Now all that could mean was that she was a snob for fine dining. But he hadn't gotten that impression about her. And she'd recommended the café first thing. He was even more curious about Amanda Cramer, and intrigued enough to even want to attend a committee meeting held by little old ladies.

THAT EVENING, AFTER three changes of clothing, Amanda ended up in sandals, white jeans—her skinny ones didn't quite fit, dammit—and a pink, cross-draped sleeveless shirt. With her hair down and wavy around her shoulders, she thought she at last looked presentable.

But she was still nervous. She'd certainly liked Mason when they'd been sitting side by side on the deck and she'd looked longingly at his mouth.

Maybe he was taking pity on her.

She groaned aloud. Where had her self-confidence gone?

She went down to the dining room and busied herself laying out the peach pie, linen napkins, china plates, and coffee cups, even though she'd only have one guest to-night. Just as she finished adding more water to the Keurig coffeemaker, she heard a sound behind her and whirled.

Mason, all dark hair and eyes, leaned against the door-jamb, the pearl buttons on his Western shirt gleaming in the shaft of sunlight coming through the lace curtains. His jeans were slung low and hugged his hips, and she couldn't help following the long line down to the toes of his brown cowboy boots.

She swallowed heavily. God, he was beautiful, and he was looking at her like some people look at peach pie. She felt another pang of doubt. She was a little too chubby, a little too tall—surely people would think they looked strange together.

She forced a smile. "Hi."

"Hi. You ready?"

"I am." She grabbed her purse from the dining room table.

He glanced at the pie. "Looks—and smells—really good."

"Thanks. You can have some when you get back."

He smacked his lips. "I might eat the whole thing."

"If you could actually do that, I'd bake you another."

He smiled down at her, dark eyes crinkling at the cor-ners. "I'll hold you to that."

If she had to bake another pie just for him, maybe he'd be in the kitchen with her, leaning up against the counter, standing too close, sex appeal on a stick. She veered away from that distracting thought.

They walked through the house and out the front door.

The street was deserted, but she felt watched. Reminding herself that the paparazzi had stopped stalking her years ago, she walked down the stairs and across Nellie Street, then headed north on Second.

"Is that the community center at the end of the block?" Mason asked. "It looks like a brick factory."

"It once was," she said. "They converted it into a center with conference rooms, a game room, and a big reception room where you can even have a small wedding. That's probably where our meeting will be tonight."

There were cars parallel-parked on the street and in the big parking lot behind the center. Groups of people crossed the deck and headed through the double doors, chatting with easy comfort. There would be a lot of people in there, people she didn't know, or people who might know her or her story. Several clustered in the doorway, as if it was already difficult to find a seat. She imagined the crowd, having to squeeze past people . . . a sudden wave of nausea made her briefly close her eyes. This was *not* going to happen again, she told herself, inhaling deeply and letting it out.

"Mason, if you don't mind, I'd like to sit by the door." Her voice sounded faint, even to her own ears.

He was studying her with true concern shadowing his eyes, but all he said was, "Sure."

Thank God the last row was totally empty, and she sank onto a folding chair, grateful that everyone else faced forward and didn't look at her—except Mrs. Palmer at the front of the room, who beamed and waved at them both, causing several people to turn with curiosity to stare at her.

Amanda's heart thumped against her ribs, as if trying to escape. When the people turned back to the front again, one by one, she told herself she could control her reaction. It wasn't like D.C., where cameramen and microphone booms had crowded her and reporters had shouted insulting questions.

She'd been thinking about it too much lately, with the five-year anniversary of the Senate hearings coming up. A reporter, Melissa Shaw, had even called from CNN, claiming she was doing a piece on women in the workplace, what had changed and what hadn't. But as usual, Amanda had said, "No comment." She wanted to forget that part of her life, and she wished the media would, too.

There had to be close to fifty people inside the community center by the time Mrs. Thalberg called the meeting to order. Amanda continued breathing evenly and told herself to concentrate on the brush of Mason's warm arm against hers. She wasn't alone, and a panic attack would only last minutes. She would get through this.

The widows took turns presenting the schedule of the Wild West Weekend on a projected computer screen. It would be held Friday and Sunday, bookending the rodeo, and include a historic tour of Valentine, where tourists could get their special passbooks stamped at each venue. A full passbook entered them in a drawing for a prize at the end. To get a passbook, a donation had to be made to the preservation fund. Vendors with carts would be selling food, and restaurants were encouraged to mimic nineteenth-century menus. Volunteers would be patrolling the streets in costume to help tourists.

After a question-and-answer period, the widows ended the meeting by pointing out the rack of costumes people could choose from if they hadn't gotten their own. There was a rush toward the rack, and Amanda found herself perspiring.

"Yoo-hoo, Amanda, come see what we have!" Mrs. Palmer called, an old-fashioned bonnet barely able to encompass her big blond wig.

Amanda couldn't take a deep enough breath. Her biggest fear, that she'd panic again like she had in D.C., seemed to be yawning toward her, and she teetered on an abyss. Her chest was constricted, her stomach bile seemed to bubble.

And then she felt the firm grip of a masculine hand taking her clammy one in his own.

"Hey, hey, everything's all right, Amanda," Mason said calmly, gently. "Turn your head and look at me."

She did and found herself staring hard into his black eyes, desperate to find something, anything to focus on other than her nausea and trembling.

"Take some deep breaths. Go ahead, breathe in, deep as you can. Come on, you can do it."

It was like her lungs had collapsed and wouldn't allow a breath of air through, though she'd been concentrating hard on staying composed. She almost sounded like she was wheezing, but she did her best.

"Okay, let it out now, nice and slow."

Quivering, she forced air from her lungs and brought more in.

"Just look in my eyes. No one is paying any attention at all. It's just us."

She nodded, but couldn't manage the words that would dismiss his concern, that would gloss over what was happening to her.

"Have you had a panic attack before?" he asked conversationally.

His fingers were massaging her hands, and it felt . . . nice.

"Y-yes," she murmured through quivering lips. "I've been working hard to make sure it wouldn't happen again."

"So you know what's going on. I don't need to have you checked out for a heart attack." He smiled gently.

She tried to return it, but her trembling lips wouldn't move as she wanted.

"So . . . so stupid," she murmured, breathing and breathing. "I need to get out of here."

She lurched to her feet, but he didn't let go of her hand.

"The door's right here," he said, leading her toward it. "Let's go admire the sunset."

On the deck, amidst the flowers and ferns, she started feeling better, and a warm evening breeze made her close her eyes and just breathe.

"You want to sit down?" he asked.

She shook her head as angry tears filled her eyes. "No," she whispered, then had to clear her throat. "Sorry, I need to walk. I feel like such a fool . . ."

She tried to remove her hand from his, but he didn't let her.

"Then let's walk. Isn't there a park just down the creek from you? Let's go there."

The park was only a few blocks away. Mason steered

her away from the gazebo, where people sat and talked on several benches, until they found a more secluded area overlooking the creek. Sitting down, he pulled her with him. When he released her hand, she clutched hers together. She raised her eyes and focused on the creek, the tree crookedly bent over it, water tumbling over shallow rocks with a soothing bubbling.

"You sound like you're breathing better," he said at last.

"I am. I know I'm supposed to focus on deep breathing. After it . . . after it happened the first time, I did a lot of research to prepare myself in case it happened again. During my first panic attack, I was being pressed in on all sides by a crowd of—of people. It was awful to have no one to help, to feel so alone and on display and to lose control." She shuddered and briefly closed her eyes, before turning toward him. "But your calmness really helped. How did you know what to do?"

"My aunt used to suffer from panic attacks, so I recognized the signs. And just so you know, one of the worst things you can do is to retreat from the situations that trigger the attack. Then it's easy to keep imagining the worst, making it even more significant and scary for you."

"I know," she said wearily. "A couple months back I started realizing I was letting fear get to me. I avoided crowds, avoided going out."

He nodded. "The servers at the café you sent me to say you've never been by."

She stiffened. "So you're talking to people about me?"

"I just wanted them to know you'd given them business by suggesting that I come for dinner there."

"Sorry." Amanda sighed. "I used to say I didn't like to eat out alone, but I realized I was fooling myself." She fisted her hands and whispered fiercely, "I hate crowds. I hate being stared at. It was a blow to discover that I was still letting it affect me so much."

"Have you always hated crowds?"

She laughed bitterly. "No, I was a lawyer. I was *good* with crowds." She almost started blurting out her past, then stopped. "I was nervous all day getting ready for this stupid meeting. I feel so foolish, so weak. I know what I'm supposed to do if it happens again, I told myself to let the panic wash over me, to calm myself, but . . . it's been years since I had a panic attack. I thought it was in my past, and to have a relapse like this . . ."

"Is this why you didn't want to do the Wild West Weekend?"

"I don't know. Maybe. God, probably. I like meeting new people—but on my own terms."

"Which is why you like having guests who go about their own business and then leave."

"I don't ignore them!" she insisted.

"I can tell. I certainly felt welcomed and at home."

She slumped back against the bench. "I realized a few months back that I started making the B&B my own little prison."

He remained silent, which gave her time to think about all the trips to the grocery store she'd assigned her assistant, Erin. Amanda had gone from browsing antique shops to checking eBay online, telling herself it was a better use of her time. She'd stayed wrapped up in her own little B&B world, never letting herself realize what had been happening to her.

"I did a lot of research and realized I was slowly turning into an agoraphobe," she confessed. "My garden was becoming my last 'safe' place outside. I realized I had to get a grip on this. I thought I was doing better, running errands, forcing myself to confront tricky situations head on. And then tonight—another attack. Dammit."

"Do you know what triggered the first one? Telling me about it might help."

She looked up at him, saw the concern and gentleness in his dark eyes.

"I . . . I don't usually talk about it."

"I'm a good listener."

She took a deep breath, and the words just burst from her. "I was the victim of sexual harassment. I hated being a victim, but this time, I'm doing it to myself."

Chapter 4

MASON STARED AT Amanda, trying to keep his shock and sadness hidden, knowing she wouldn't welcome it. He couldn't imagine someone abusing her; it gave him a dark, tense upheaval in his gut that made him want to punish the man who'd caused her suffering.

"Amanda, I'm so sorry," he said, taking her hand again. He was relieved she allowed it, and their linked hands rested between them on the bench. "You can talk to me."

"It happened at work." She winced. "I just thought he was a flirt—some guys are."

"Your boss?"

"Yeah. He was friendly with everyone, you know? And that's why people didn't believe me when I had to tell the truth. Everyone was convinced I was misreading his 'friendliness,'" she said, using air quotes. "When I turned down his requests for dinner, he started brushing up against me too frequently to be accidental. God, he made my flesh crawl by the end of it. What was I going to say to people—'His arm brushed mine'?"

She sounded so angry, bitter, and sad. He realized she'd left behind her career—one she'd worked hard for—because of this man.

"But it got worse," she said hoarsely. "He got me alone once at the end of the day, when I hadn't realized we were the only ones in the office. He tried to force a kiss on me, and I only got away by giving him a good knee to the balls, grabbing my shoulder bag, and running."

"Good for you. The scum deserved it," Mason said fiercely. "Is that when you came forward?"

She shook her head. "I was already applying for a new job to get away from him. But then he threatened to fire me, to blacken my name if I didn't have sex with him. That's when I went public. To face a whole panel of his supporters and all those cameras . . ." She shuddered.

Confused, he gave her hand a gentle squeeze. "What do you mean, cameras were involved?"

"Oh, I forgot to explain that part, did I?" she said bitterly. "My boss was a United States senator."

Mason clenched his jaw until his teeth ground together, but he controlled his outward reaction. It was obvious she hadn't spoken of the harassment in a long time, for the words were pouring out of her.

"I had no proof, never thought to record what he'd done—I just wanted to get away from him. But he made that impossible, and I couldn't let that go or let that happen to other women. When I complained, they opened an investigation, and I ended up having to testify in front of an ethics panel. It was . . . awful. There was nothing but my word, and it wasn't good enough."

"He got away with it?" Mason asked, appalled.

"For a while. I resigned. The publicity, the reporters—it was just too much. They followed me everywhere I went, trying to get me to recant or say something new and explosive. People I thought were my friends turned against me. I lasted another year in D.C., but my life was hell, and my new employer was using me like a poster child for fighting the establishment. At the one-year anniversary, it all came up again, and that's when . . . when I had my first panic attack. Cameras and microphones in my face—they had me backed into a corner."

He could see her pale face flush, feel the tremble in her hand as she remembered.

"I didn't think I'd be able to get away. I didn't faint or anything. I forced myself to watch the clip on TV later and I looked distressed, but not incapacitated, thank God. I gave it all up and went home to Denver, to my parents. I hid out for a while, even after another woman came forward and told what the senator did to her. She'd been smart enough to record it, and he ended up quitting politics."

"I remember a senator resigning in disgrace a few years back."

She nodded. "I hope he's never in a position to do that to a woman again. But as for me—I was done with Washington. I worked at a small law firm in Denver for a couple years, but my heart wasn't in it. I had enough saved up to take some time and discover what I wanted to do. I came to Aspen to do some skiing, but I didn't want to stay in a big hotel where I might be recognized. That's when I tried my first B&B and fell in love with it. I found and bought Connections a year ago now, and I've never been happier." Her lips twisted with sarcasm. "And then I realized I've been using my home just to hide."

"I don't believe that," he said. "You're good at what you do—it's obvious you love it."

She sighed. "Thanks. I have a lot of help from my assistant innkeeper, Erin. One of the ways I realized I was in trouble was that I'd only leave my house with Erin, someone I trust. And tonight, I went out with you."

He stared at her in surprise. "You trust me?"

"I . . . I don't know what it is about you or why, but . . . yeah, I guess I must trust you."

They stared at each other a long moment, and the setting sun just dipping behind the mountains highlighted her blushing cheeks. Those dark blue eyes were like crystal windows into her turbulent emotions. And he was fascinated. She was a woman who'd come through some of the worst moments imaginable, still suffered the effects, and yet she'd succeeded in owning her own business.

"I hope that doesn't make you leery," she continued. "I wouldn't blame you if you wanted to run far away from someone with my kind of problems."

"I think you're strong and brave, and you've already taken steps to improve your life. So you had a little setback tonight. It doesn't negate the fact that you stood up against a powerful man with only your word."

"Other people might call me stupid."

"Not me—and not yourself."

She bit her lip, and for the first time in hours, he saw a glimpse of her sweet smile.

"Yeah, I couldn't let him get away with it," she said. "Even at the height of the craziness, I didn't regret that I'd told the truth. And when I was vindicated—it was a good feeling. But the resulting notoriety? Not something most people would like. Thankfully, you'll never know what it feels like to have so many people staring, judging."

He felt the first stirrings of unease. He knew what it was like, of course, though he'd only been famous within the rodeo world. But there was a big difference—she was trying to forget about her fame, and he was trying to use his to attract an investor. It felt a little cheap—but it was necessary. It didn't feel right to bring it up, as if comparing their situations, when there was no comparison at all.

"About this Wild West Weekend," Amanda said. "It's a little ironic that I bought a place where women were exploited. I'm proof things haven't changed all that much."

He squinted at her. "Things have changed—and you helped change them by speaking out. That wouldn't have happened a hundred years ago."

She shrugged, smiling.

"You've decided to participate?"

"I have. I can't avoid the things that make me anxious; I've been working hard to face them and get through them, and make myself realize that I can. I'm used to people coming into my house—this'll be no different."

"I can't wait to see what costume you choose," he said.

She raised an eyebrow.

He laughed. "Think your other guests might want to join in?"

"I don't know. I'll ask when they arrive. But I might rope you in."

He let go of her hand to raise both of his. "Not as a john."

She laughed. "How about as the sheriff, come to make sure customers don't cause trouble?"

His grin spread across his face. "I like that. Sheriff Lopez. Bet there weren't many sheriffs with that kind of last name in the old west."

Her expression sobered. "Yet you have important business here besides the rodeo. You don't have to participate, Mason."

"But I want to. I may not be around all day, but get me a badge, Madam."

She smiled, watching him out of the corner of her eye almost shyly. "I guess we should get back."

"There's still that drink I promised you."

She hesitated, and he wasn't surprised when at last she shook her head.

"If you don't mind, I'll pass. I need some time to think about what happened tonight, to prepare myself for tomorrow."

"I understand. Maybe a rain check?"

"We'll see."

"Then at least let me walk home with you, since we're going to the same place."

"I'd like that. And you still need a piece of peach pie."

"Believe me, I haven't forgotten."

They shared another smile and turned to walk across the grass, elbows brushing. He took her hand again, and although she shot him a startled look, she didn't pull away.

Chapter 5

IN THE MORNING, Amanda did the yoga stretches she'd begun a couple months ago as part of her recovery. The garden was the perfect peaceful setting, and she felt wonderful watching the sun rise over the mountains. As she lay on her back on a mat, relaxing and breathing deeply, she thought of Mason Lopez, his kindness and concern. She wouldn't have blamed him if he'd packed up and left. It had been a long time since she'd felt excited about a man—years, in fact. She'd dated a few times in Denver but had never felt a spark, not like this one.

And . . . it scared her.

Yet it was her job to provide Mason with breakfast. Though feeling nervous, she took a quick shower, then took special care with her makeup and hair, like she was going out on a date instead of serving her guest a meal and then running errands.

She'd given Erin the day off, so it was just her in her

kitchen. Though she'd given the space some old-fashioned touches, like lace curtains and antique kitchen tools hung on the walls, her working space was modern to the core— granite counters, an industrial mixer, several large waffle makers. She'd frozen homemade muffin batter in individual liners and taken several out to thaw last night. Now she popped them into the oven, and the smell soon filled the whole downstairs.

In the dining room, she was at the sideboard laying out a fresh fruit salad, several cereal selections, yogurt, and granola bars, when she heard the squeak of footsteps on the front stairs. She felt an electric shock buzz through her, and when Mason appeared a moment later, she told herself to give him just a professional smile. But it was difficult, when he made her feel so full of yearning and regret. He was wearing another perfectly pressed Western checked shirt with his jeans. To think she'd once thought a man in a suit the height of sexiness.

He smiled in return. "Mornin', Amanda."

She liked the sound of her name in that deep, masculine voice. It rumbled right through her, and she had to squelch a shiver. "Hi, Mason," she said, hearing a little breathlessness and feeling silly.

"No chocolates on my pillow last night?" he teased.

"If I did that and you didn't see them, you'd wake up with chocolate in your hair."

He chuckled.

And then she remembered her job. "I'll have some fresh muffins for you in a moment. Until then, please help yourself. Would you like coffee? I can bring a French press."

"That would be great, thanks."

"Today's hot breakfast is a ham and cheese quiche. Would you like that?"

"I'll take some of anything you've got."

She blushed, wondering if he was actually flirting with her.

He looked around at her dining room, and she saw it through his eyes: the gold wallpaper, the chandelier, the glass-fronted cabinets displaying her nineteenth-century china collection, the lace tablecloth covering her mahogany table and displaying place settings for six. She'd thrown the French doors wide to catch the morning breeze.

"You could eat on the porch if you'd like," she said, gesturing to the tables for two or four people.

"Naw, that's okay. It's nice right here. You'll be joining me, right?"

"I don't usually disturb my guests while they eat."

"But this guest is all alone."

She knew she should refuse. And then she heard herself saying, "All right. Help yourself"—she gestured to the sideboard—"while I fetch your muffins."

Wincing at her own giddy foolishness, she brought the cloth-lined basket, brimming with a selection of blueberry, bran, and apple muffins. She also set down a plate of butter pats, molded into flower shapes.

He blinked in surprise. "Wow. You really go all out."

"That's the point of a B&B, isn't it?"

Ten minutes later, she brought out two plates with wedges of quiche steaming upon them.

Mason inhaled. "Can't wait to dig in. Please join me."

So she did, perpendicular to his right, since he'd taken the head of the table that looked out on the yard. Blue sat on a chair in the corner and just watched them, tail swishing lazily. They ate and talked about nothing in particular, mostly about quaint small towns, comparing Valentine Valley and Elk's Crest. Safe subjects, Amanda thought.

When a lengthier silence fell, he said, "I saw you in the garden this morning."

Damn her pale, blushing complexion.

He rushed on. "I'm usually up before dawn. Hard to break old habits. It's just . . . I happened to look out just as the sun crested the Sawatch mountains, and it seemed to . . . ripple across you, patterned through the trees. It was peaceful and beautiful."

To her surprise, her eyes moistened, and she wished she could see herself like he did. To make light of her over-reaction, she said, "What are you, a cowboy poet?"

"Shucks, no," he said, shrugging and digging back into his quiche with gusto. "Was that yoga you were doing?"

"Yeah, I feel so much better afterward, relaxed and strong."

"I can tell you take care of yourself," he said, dark eyes warm with what could only be admiration.

Flustered now, she said, "And meditation. That's important, too."

"I've done some meditating."

"You have?"

"Sure. Only I'm usually on the back of a horse, riding slowly, enjoying the quiet. Can you call that meditation?"

"I think so. As long as you clear your mind and only think about your breathing for a while, you're set."

"It's hard to think of nothing, when there's always so much to do."

"I hear you," she said, rising to her feet to take his plate, glad for the excuse to escape his sweetness and her reluctant attraction.

"Let me help," he said, starting to stand.

"No way. You're my guest. Have another muffin or some yogurt."

"Yes, ma'am," he said, eyeing the sideboard with interest.

When she returned to the dining room fifteen minutes later, Mason was still there, reading the *Valentine Gazette*, which she'd left out for guests.

"There's a big article on the Wild West Weekend, along with the rodeo," he said. "You still going to give it a try?"

"Yep, I'm calling the Widows' Boardinghouse after breakfast."

"Good for you. Does that include the rodeo, too?"

When unease stirred inside her like scurrying mice, she brushed it aside. "Yes, I'm coming. I won't let last night affect my recovery. But I do have to work first."

He gestured to the paper. "Take a look at the schedule. I ride late in the morning."

She came to look over his shoulder and saw the bull-riding schedule, but soon the warmth of his broad back so close to her chest distracted her too much to read.

He glanced sideways at her, which brought his face inches from hers. She turned her head to face him, knowing she should straighten up, back away. But . . . she couldn't. It was like she was frozen in place, desire overwhelming good sense. It had been years since a man had made her feel this way, daring and reckless, and she was caught off guard.

He leaned toward her, his movements slow and easy, giving her plenty of time to back away. But she didn't, only waited in anticipation for the brush of his lips on hers. And it was a gentle brush, as if her lips had been the delicate petals of flowers that would bend in the slightest wind.

But she wasn't delicate, she told herself, and leaned into the kiss, parting her lips to taste him, to explore the fullness of his lower lip.

With a groan, he turned, and before she knew it, she was lying across his lap and he was holding her tightly against him. His mouth slanted across hers, hot and inviting and arousing. When their tongues met, it was her turn to moan her welcome. She plunged her hand into his hair, feeling the silkiness of dark curls, while her other arm slid up his back. She could feel the tension in his muscles as he held her, while she felt positively urgent with passion and need, as if she couldn't get close enough.

At last he lifted his head and looked down at her, breathing hard. Wide-eyed, she stared back at him, her wet lips parted.

"I hope you don't need an apology for that," he said huskily.

"You better not apologize" was her fierce response.

He briefly hugged her close. "I would keep on kissing you, but I have an appointment, and you have things to do, too. And there's still that drink we didn't have."

Almost shaky with the aftermath of such intense, conflicted feelings, Amanda slowly sat up. Perched on his knee, she couldn't help looking deep into his black eyes. "We both have so much to do. I don't think we could fit in a drink—"

"I won't accept no for an answer." His grin was slow in coming, white teeth gleaming in his tanned face. "But if you're going to do the Wild West Weekend tomorrow, you might have a lot of prep to do tonight. Squeeze me in?"

"I'll try."

His smile changed into an earnest look as he cupped her face in his hands and kissed her once more.

AFTER CALLING THE widows, Amanda took fifteen minutes to meditate. To her relief, Mason had gone, so she was able to clean and tidy his room. She was never nosy with her guests, but she couldn't help noticing how neatly he'd folded away his clothes, how he'd even wiped the sink after shaving. And then she escaped before she could moon over him anymore. She had errands to run. The Sassafras Girls would be arriving that afternoon, and although their rooms were ready, she wanted to be back in plenty of time, working on the Wild West Weekend transformation.

During the quick drive to the community center, she remembered her panic attack, but tried not to dwell on it. There would be no large crowd there—just the widows and a few costumes to choose from before moving on. Still, when she entered the doors to the reception room, she felt a little light-headed at the bad memories, but let the feeling pass over her and concentrated on her breathing. She would conquer this.

The room seemed deserted, with chairs folded up after the previous night's meeting, but rows of costumes still hung on several freestanding clothes racks. Sadly, the selection seemed much thinner, and she hoped she hadn't waited too long.

"Amanda!"

She gave a start, only to see Mrs. Palmer step out from behind the nearest clothes rack, wearing the simple cloth dress, bonnet, and apron of a prairie settler.

Amanda smiled. "Hi, Mrs. Palmer. You're certainly ready for the Wild West Weekend."

Mrs. Palmer did a spry little twirl. "I do enjoy dressin' up. Sorry the others couldn't meet up with us."

"Oh, no, I'm grateful you could make time for me at all."

"I must admit, you've been surprisin' me a lot these last couple days. I was surprised—but pleased!—to see you here last night, surprised to see you run off like you'd been chased out of Dodge by the sheriff, and completely surprised when you called this mornin'."

Amanda felt her cheeks heat with embarrassment. "I know, and I'm sorry that I seemed so indecisive. It's just that . . ." She trailed off, not knowing if she should explain herself. It was so humiliating to be afraid of what other people took for granted. Taking a deep breath, she met the old woman's kind eyes. "I just . . . have trouble being in crowds, and last night, it was particularly bad."

Mrs. Palmer touched her shoulder. "I thought it might

be somethin' like that. Either that, or you were about to lose your dinner!"

Amanda gave a wan smile. "It felt like that, trust me. But the Wild West Weekend can be part of my recovery."

"Well, I won't ask what happened in your past, don't you worry. I'm just glad you'll be participatin'. I did put Connections on the special map we made—I just had a good feelin' you'd change your mind."

They picked out a freestanding sign to set on her sidewalk marking her B&B as another stop on the tour. Amanda explained her ideas of how to entertain visitors, and Mrs. Palmer was gleeful as she promised to stop by and see the fun. Then she showed Amanda the passbook that guests would be using, and when she offered up a generic star as the stamp representing Connections, the crafter in Amanda gave herself the challenge to find something to better represent her B&B.

Lastly, they roamed the clothes racks together, and this was where Amanda's indecisiveness had cost her. "Uh-oh, I'm not sure there's anything I can wear."

"Sure there is. And if it's a little too big, you can pin it in the back."

Mrs. Palmer held up a low-cut, red satin dress with tiny straps and full skirt that fell all the way to the floor, cinching in at the waist.

"Families might be coming in," Amanda said, shaking her head. "That neckline—"

"Haven't you ever heard of a strategically placed lace handkerchief?" Mrs. Palmer pulled one from up her sleeve and put it in Amanda's hands. "This is fresh and clean, I promise. Now I heard you're havin' the Sassafras Girls as guests. I set aside some saloon girl dresses just in case they want to play along. And of course, there's that nice young rancher stayin' at your place. Did you have somethin' in mind for him?"

Could Mrs. Palmer read the infatuation in her hot face? She cleared her throat. "Something in mind . . . ?"

"Surely he'll want to dress up!"

"Oh! Oh, of course. He said he'd be the sheriff making sure everything was okay at the 'disorderly house.' That's what they sometimes called brothels."

"Ooh, you've done your research! I'm sure I can find somethin' in this box to help."

They dug in and ended up finding a tin badge, a holster, and plastic gun.

"And I saw he can provide his own cowboy hat," Mrs. Palmer added, her bright eyes watching Amanda too closely.

Amanda loaded up her car with costumes and prayed she wasn't asking too much of her guests—or herself. Then she spent several hours scouring stores in Valentine, Basalt, and Carbondale until she had everything she needed. Her nerves surfaced a bit when Hal's Hardware had a dozen customers just getting out of a how-to-paint class, but she let them jostle past her on their way out, reminding herself that no one knew her, no one was paying attention, no one could read "panic disorder" on her forehead. She knew her anxiety wasn't gone—it would take a lot more than a couple of errands to convince her that last night was a rare exception to her recovery. She'd recently spent time talking with a counselor, too, and she'd make a follow-up appointment next week.

All in all, as she tossed the last item in her trunk, she was feeling pretty confident about herself.

Until she saw Mason across the street, waving to her. She waved back, feeling a mixture of embarrassment and pleasure as she remembered their kiss. But no, she couldn't let herself make more of this than it was: a flirtation with a cowboy who was going home.

Then he crossed the street and headed for her.

Chapter 6

When Mason saw Amanda on the street, he felt a rush of happiness and pleasure and satisfaction all rolled together. He was happy just watching her ponytail bob as she walked to meet him. And the pleasure—he'd barely been able to concentrate on his meeting that morning, for remembering the hot kiss they'd shared.

They both came to a stop facing each other, a little closer than was necessary. He almost swept her up in a hug but thought better of it.

"Hi," he said, unable to stop grinning.

A blush pinkened her cheeks, and she didn't quite meet his gaze. "Hi."

He lowered his voice. "I almost kissed you right here on the street as if I had a right to."

She seemed to redden even more. A lock of hair had come loose from her ponytail, and he tucked it behind her ear slowly. He thought he detected a shiver.

"There," he murmured. "I was just about to get some lunch. Want to join me? You do owe me a date." He stuck out his elbow.

She hesitated, staring at his arm but not touching.

He waited, as if the rest of his life could be affected by Amanda's decision to trust him. He wanted to be with her; he'd never met another woman who so fascinated him. "We'll go to Tony's Tavern. It's off the tourist track, and the locals know how to mind their own business."

"Since when?" she said lightly.

But to his relief, she slid her arm into his. He smiled. "Valentine Valley can't be as full of busybodies as Elk's Crest. Surely there have to be some strangers down here."

"Guess I'm a stranger to most people around here," she said. "And you've met the widows—we have our busybodies. But okay, I'll go and check out the tavern. I've always heard good things."

"Yep, saw it on your restaurant list."

"How about if I drive you to Tony's? My car is full of stuff. And later I can drive you back to wherever your pickup is."

He grinned. "All so I can drive the couple blocks to my next appointment."

"Small towns," she said, shaking her head.

At Tony's, there were a few people at tables within the dark bar. Flat-screen TVs alternated with mounted animal heads on the walls. A back room featured a pool table, where Mason had played once or twice. But none of that mattered as he focused all his attention on Amanda. He closed the door, shutting out the July heat. She tossed a smile over her shoulder at him, and it set off his own hot simmer.

Though a sign said to wait to be seated, the bartender, a guy in his early thirties with longish brown hair that touched the collar of his black polo shirt, gestured for them to pick a table. When the bartender was finished bringing an order of food to another table, he introduced himself as the owner, Tony, and they placed a drink order. Amanda stopped him before he could leave.

"I already know what I want," she said, closing her menu. "I'll take a burger and coleslaw."

"I like a woman who knows her own mind," Tony said, smiling.

"I'll take the same," Mason said, "except make mine French fries."

Tony nodded. "I'll be back with your drinks."

"So tell me about your meeting," Amanda said to Mason.

He leaned back in the wooden chair. "Our ranch is bringing stock—calves, steer, horses, and bulls—for the rodeo this weekend, so I wanted to make sure the local ranchers came out and saw what we have. There's a national-level bull I want to buy to really improve our stock, but unless I come up with an investor, I can't swing the loan on my own, not with the problems my dad accidentally caused."

"Bulls cost that much?"

"Bulls with this kind of lineage and track record do. A cattle company can be made on the success of good breeders. I can't tell you how much of my daily thoughts are about which of my cows I'd cross with that bull to produce the perfect bucker."

"Ah, those are your thoughts when you insist you're meditating," she said, giving him a sly grin.

He snorted. "I have time for those thoughts, too, trust me." He glanced down at the shadow of cleavage produced when she leaned forward. In a softer voice, he said, "I have time for other thoughts, too."

She dropped her gaze, and he couldn't tell if he'd embarrassed her or not. She sat back as Tony set her Diet Coke in front of her, and a beer bottle in front of Mason.

When Tony had gone, Amanda turned a serious expression on him. "How old are you, Mason?"

"Thirty-three."

"I'm thirty-four. I'm not ever going to be a regular girl like the ones you've dated in the past."

"And you know all about my past?" He lightened his tone, attempting to tease, but he was curious where she was going with this.

"No, but . . . I have issues. You already know about them, so that's good. But . . . with all you've got going on, with the ranch and your dad . . . you don't need to deal with someone like me."

He opened his mouth, but she held up a hand.

"Just hear me out," she continued. "We've kissed, and it was good, really good. And I don't mean to sound like I'm assuming we'll have more, but . . . I've given this a lot of thought. I would understand if you want to stop right here, before things get serious." She winced. "Damn, I'm really making a lot of assumptions here. Maybe to you I sound arrogant or—"

"No, you don't. I know you think you're protecting me or something, but you can stop. Do you think we're all so perfect compared to you?"

She blinked at him. "Of course not. But Mason, I have issues that won't go away overnight."

"This may be our first official date, but I promise we can still take things as slow as you need to. Give us a chance."

She studied him for a long time, until they were interrupted by Tony bringing their burgers. Tony set the plates down, looked between them, then backed away slowly, hands upraised.

Amanda chuckled, her expression relaxing. As she cut her burger in half, she said, "Mason, I've laid my cards on the table. I don't know how else to be plainer."

"I'm glad to know where we stand. We're getting to know each other; that's what dating is about. And then if you decide we should only be friends, I'll accept it."

"You will?" she whispered, her eyes soft on him.

"I will. But I still think we're destined for more."

AMANDA WAS GLAD she could use the Wild West Weekend to escape her conflicted thoughts about Mason. She called Erin back to work, and the two of them dove into the decorating and baking. When Mason returned from his dinner out, he tried to join in, but she refused, saying he was a guest, and it was nice enough of him to participate a couple of hours tomorrow afternoon. She kept a folding screen up and the lights low to block most of his view of the parlor. After giving him his holster, gun, and badge, she shooed him off to his room.

She hoped he didn't think she was trying to get rid of him, but . . . she sort of was. His very presence was distracting, making her forget she shouldn't be focusing on flirtation when she had so much work to do.

The four Sassafras Girls checked in, totally thrilled to be asked to participate in the Wild West Weekend. They oohed and giggled over their costumes, and even offered to play a song or two every half hour for the afternoon, which would allow Amanda to host house tours in between. But Amanda wanted them to have fun in town, too, so they agreed they'd alternate their participation with only two of them at a time hanging out as saloon girls.

By the time Amanda collapsed into bed at one in the morning, she assumed she was too tired to think about anything. But that powerful kiss with Mason lingered in her dreams.

Chapter 7

MASON HAD TO spend the morning at the Silver Creek Ranch, meeting up with his sisters and making sure their livestock was settled in preparation for the next day's rodeo. Other contractors were there as well, so although he saw Nate Thalberg from a distance, he didn't get a chance to talk to the busy man. Mason was going to have to win tomorrow to get any kind of notice. He was feeling pretty confident when he returned to Connections around eleven. He had to grin at the sign on the front lawn, advertising the B&B as a stop for Valentine Valley's Wild West Weekend.

Inside, he came to a stop and simply gaped. The curtains were now covered by a fall of red velvet draped over the rods. There were oil lamps on the tables, candles on the mantel, and the recorded sounds of a player piano in the background. Brochures were spread on an end table in the hall, advertising the Wild West Weekend, as well as

Connections B&B. A round table with a deck of cards and poker chips sat in the middle of the floor. Amanda's cat, Blue, curled its way around the table legs.

And at that table, playing poker, were two strangers in saloon girl clothes, satin bodices over frilly skirts that ended around their knees. Near at hand rested a guitar, which reminded him who these ladies were: Sassafras Girls, playing their part, grinning and flashing him some thigh.

He tipped his cowboy hat to them both.

"How does it all look?"

He turned around at the sound of Amanda's voice, and his mouth dropped open. She was dressed in red satin with black trim that fell in languid folds to the floor. It hugged all her curves in a way that made it difficult for him to swallow. At the neckline, white lace obscured any plummeting depths. He swallowed.

She smiled shyly and did a little twirl. "Howdy, Sheriff."

He cleared his throat, although he still sounded hoarse as he said, "Howdy, ma'am."

"You can call me Miss Amanda. Glad you're here. These girls are gettin' too uppity for me."

The "girls" laughed aloud, and Amanda took his arm and pulled him back into the hall.

"Did you see this sign advertising our wares?" she said in her normal voice, now laced with excitement. "It'll go right over a kid's head, won't it?"

She pointed to a rough piece of paper tacked on the wall that read:

Hot under the Collar: 10 cents
Starch in Shorts: 50 cents
Remove Starch from Shorts: $1
All payment in advance. High Grade silver ore will be accepted.

Mason laughed. "That's perfect. And I like the piano music, too."

She winced. "I ended up downloading that. It was hard to find something just right in the small CD section of the Open Book. Did you look in the corner?" She pointed to a miner's pickax resting next to silver rocks. "I sprayed the rocks with paint."

She was filled with such exuberance that he couldn't take his eyes off her. This was a woman who knew how to enjoy life, to make her own fun, but she'd been hiding out too long in fear.

"I even have a dartboard for guests to try," she said, pointing to the board next to the mantel. "Of course, it's magnetic. Can't have holes in my walls. Come on and see the food we're serving."

She led him through the library to the dining room, where a woman in a plain skirt, blouse, and apron was carrying out a tray.

"Erin, this is our guest, Mason Lopez, but you can call him 'Sheriff' today."

The woman put down the tray and they shook hands. Erin was in her forties, with short, curly black hair and green eyes that looked upon Amanda in almost a motherly way.

"What do you think about the food?" Amanda asked, sliding her arm into his so naturally. "We tried to make it as authentic as we could."

The display included cornbread, pork and beans, biscuits and gravy, mini chicken pot pies, and bread pudding, served along with apple cider and coffee. All of it was offered in appetizer-sized portions.

As he was beginning to take a piece here and there, Amanda looked at the watch face pinned to her chest.

"Oh, it's almost eleven thirty. Time for another house tour."

"They've been going well?"

"It's only my second, but I love talking about the history of my home."

"How did it get to be a brothel if it was first built as someone's home?"

"When the silver market collapsed, the owners lost everything and abandoned the place. A 'bad element' moved in," she said, using air quotes.

"So you think you'll get some new customers out of this?"

"I almost don't care. I'm having such fun!"

Grinning, he watched her walk back toward the parlor, hips swinging with exaggeration, the red satin of her dress catching the firelight of the lamps and candles.

Erin was watching her, too, but with satisfaction. "She seems so much happier than she's been in a long time."

"I'm glad," Mason said. "The widows really knew what they were doing, inviting her to participate in this weekend event."

Erin gave him a speculative glance. "I don't think it's just the widows. I spent last evening in the kitchen with her. She mentioned you a lot, Sheriff."

He cleared his throat. "Well, thanks, ma'am. But it's Miss Amanda who really shines."

"I certainly like hearing that. Now, you better go change. You can take the back staircase." She pointed into the hall outside the kitchen.

Ten minutes later, Mason came down the main staircase, taking his time and looking around, hand on his gun holster which was slung low around his hips. Amanda was talking to a half dozen people about the B&B's having been a "disorderly house" run by a con woman. He swaggered over to the poker table, straddled a chair backwards, and sent a meaningful stare at the two Sassafras Girls.

"You girls better be behavin' yourselves," he warned, maybe a bit melodramatically.

The girls, their hair at each end of the blond spectrum, wore exaggerated eye makeup and red pouting lips.

"Then you better keep us out of trouble, Sheriff," said the dark blond. "I'm Nikki, and this is Brandy. Do you play poker?"

"Do I play poker," he echoed confidently, taking the deck from her hands and shuffling.

Brandy giggled and sipped something amber-colored from an old-fashioned glass. She poured him two fingers in a glass, and when he tasted apple cider, he grinned.

The afternoon passed by almost too swiftly. Amanda worked harder than any of them, giving tours, helping Erin in the kitchen, overseeing her "girls" when they played poker. The Sassafras Girls switched out, and the next two—Danielle, a shaggy-haired brunette, and Felicia, who had close-cropped black hair—decided to give him a run for his money at darts. Danielle was a little more free with her hands, running one along his arm or shoulder, and then once pinching his ass and giving him a wicked grin when he shot her a startled look.

"Girls, nothin' given away for free to the customers— even if he is the sheriff," Amanda said sternly as she was seeing another tour group out the door. "And isn't it time for a song?"

Mason was glad to escape Danielle, who picked up her guitar, playing and singing harmony for Felicia, who had a deep, soulful voice that sounded as if she'd once sung gospel in church. The tourists who'd been sampling food in the dining room filtered back toward the parlor to listen.

Amanda slid her arm possessively into Mason's, and he pulled her down to sit on his lap. Playing her role to the hilt, she gave a low, throaty laugh.

"Miss Amanda," he crooned near her ear, "I do believe I wish it was you who'd given me an encouragin' pinch."

She laughed softly, then donned her good-time "madam" expression. "Why, Sheriff, it's my girls who earn the money here."

"I don't think I offered to pay with anything but pleasure."

She blushed and playfully tucked his arm around her waist, while they listened to the Sassafras Girls sing about lost love.

Mason hoped she knew he wasn't kidding about the pleasure.

AMANDA HAD THE best afternoon she'd experienced in a long time. Mason jumped into the playacting wholeheartedly, acting as if the sheriff was Miss Amanda's lover. He stayed by her side and teasingly warned away the occasional male tourist who tried to flirt with her. He fetched her food and drink, looked over her shoulder to give her poker tips when she played, until she was intimately aware of his warm breath on her bare shoulder.

They stayed in character so much that when Amanda brought in the street sign at seven o'clock, signaling an end to a successful day showing off Connections, he was still waiting for her, leaning against the wall, arms folded across his broad chest, cowboy hat tipped low over his eyes. The Sassafras Girls had left to explore Valentine Valley's rodeo-weekend nightlife, and Erin had gone home to her family.

It was just the two of them alone in the silence of the empty house. Shadows of the setting sun had swept across the parlor, already darkened by the red swaths of curtains. The oil lamps and candles illuminated recessed corners and hidden décor.

And suddenly she was very, very aware of the open neck of his shirt emphasizing bare skin, his rolled-up sleeves displaying veins in his forearms, evidence of hard work. The way his hips were cocked, with that gun on display, made him seem like he really was from another time, dangerous to a girl's virtue.

Not that she had any maidenly virtue. And she was playing the part of a woman who knew men well. It was . . . exciting to be someone other than herself, to pretend, just for a night, that she had everything under control, including this sensual, dark man.

When he spoke, his voice was a low, rumbling murmur meant just for her. "Miss Amanda, I do believe I could use a drink—a real one. I don't suppose you can help out a thirsty cowboy-sheriff?"

She kept her smile flirtatious. "I don't keep libation freely available in the public rooms, Sheriff. It encourages the rowdy clientele. But I do believe I have something you'd like in my private stock. Why don't you follow me?"

Deep inside, a part of her seemed to be waving her off, reminding her of her caution, but she ignored it. She and Mason were having a drink, that was all. With her hands on her hips, she swept past him and up the stairs, exaggerating the rolling motion of her walk, using her curves to all the advantage she never usually did. The folds of her satin skirt rubbed along each other with a sibilant hiss that seemed to whisper between the heavy, advancing steps of his cowboy boots.

On the second floor, she went to the back of the house through a door marked PRIVATE, where she entered another hallway. There were several doors, one to the back staircase, another to a storage closet. The third was to her bedroom, and she opened it, stepping inside and sinking into the soft rug on the wooden floor.

She treated herself, as she treated her guests, with expensive duvets and sheets. They covered the four-poster bed, which now seemed to dominate the room. She didn't look at it, and instead went to the sitting room, where gauzy curtains fluttered in the evening breeze and the scent of fresh flowers wafted over them. An antique washstand held a pitcher and basin, but on the shelf beneath were several bottles of liquor and, lower still, a small refrigerator.

"Sheriff, name your poison," she said, still exaggerating a Western drawl. She was having too much fun. "There's ice in the fridge if you need it." Okay, that wasn't exactly a historic detail.

Soon they were sitting side by side on a curved-back love seat, clinking glasses together, ice cubes tinkling, their outer thighs touching. The scotch slid down smoothly and hit her belly with a shot of heat—but it wasn't hotter than the smoking gaze he was trailing down her body.

And then he reached up and plucked the lace handkerchief out of her neckline, revealing the deep valley between her breasts. She let him look, feeling branded wherever his gaze touched.

"I *thought* that was removable," he said hoarsely.

"The dress was a little too revealing for the tour. But . . . I like how putting it on made me like a different person."

He slid closer, their hips touching now, making her take another fortifying sip of scotch.

"Different in a good way?" he asked, then slowly leaned in and pressed a kiss just beneath her ear.

She inhaled swiftly, shakily, but she didn't stop him—

didn't *want* to stop him. She was languid and aware and so desperate for his touch.

When his teeth tugged gently at her earlobe, she shuddered with pleasure and closed her eyes. It had been so long since she'd let down her guard with a man—years of self-denial, of mistrust. But Mason was a man who knew her secrets, and rather than judge her, all he'd tried to do was help. She was done retreating from life. She was young and full of passion, and she wanted to remember what that felt like.

He didn't touch her with his hands, just his mouth, sliding his moist lips down her throat, taking the occasional gentle nip that made her moan. He traced his tongue along her neckline, delving beneath to hidden, sensitive skin. Sliding her hands up to his broad, hard shoulders, she arched backward over the arm of the love seat and held him to her, feeling the warmth of his kisses between her breasts, desperate to have nothing at all separating them.

He rose over her, his chest pressing her down, his hand sliding up beneath her skirt, along the outside of her leg. She hadn't bothered with the historical accuracy of bloomers, so his touch trailed along her bare flesh, raising goose bumps in its wake. Then he hit the small string of her thong, and they both moaned.

He lifted his head and stared down at her, dark eyes narrowed, face intent with passion, while his hand cupped her hip. "Amanda, if you don't want this . . . if I'm moving too fast . . . tell me now."

But all her worries about the future had faded. There was only Mason, his sweet concern, his flattering desire, and her own desperation. She put her hands on his face, felt the faint whiskers against her palms, and pulled him to her for a deep kiss. Their mouths played, licking, exploring, teasing, until finally he boldly went deeper, meeting her tongue with his, stroking until she squirmed with need.

Her breath was coming fast now, her breasts rising and falling within the constricting dress that had been shaped to mold her best assets. He'd certainly noticed, for he went there again, pressing kisses along the smooth curves, even as he dropped to his knees on the floor, parting her legs so that he could settle his torso between.

And suddenly she could take a deep breath. The bodice gaped forward, when she hadn't even felt his hands at her back. But she didn't question it, just enjoyed the heat of arousal between her thighs when he stared at her naked breasts. He lifted one gently and put his mouth to it, flicking his tongue, taking long strokes that made her cry out her rising desperation.

His hand was moving up her inner thigh with purpose, and she found herself arching up against him, whimpering as she waited for the touch that would be magic. His fingers traced the lace along her thong, then rubbed gently across the satin right at the very heart of her. She shuddered in his arms, wanting more. He didn't deprive her, sliding his thumb beneath the lace and dipping into the hot wetness before sliding up and over her clitoris.

She cried out, legs and arms trembling. His open mouth claimed her breasts, his fingers stroked her, and within minutes she climaxed hard, shuddering beneath him, throwing her head back in triumph.

Everything inside her turned weak with satisfaction, and she half-opened her eyes, meeting his dark, smoldering gaze. He wasn't languid but tense with his own need, his hands gripping her hips. She shoved hard on his chest and he fell back onto the soft carpet before the bare fireplace, bracing on his elbows. She rose to her feet over him, holding her full skirts high, feeling powerful and alluring as he caught a glimpse beneath.

"Do you have a condom?" she asked. "I know I can find one in my room somewhere."

"In my pocket. I wasn't taking any chances. A sheriff is always prepared."

Grinning, she knelt down, straddling his thighs, letting her gown pool around her waist in red splendor. With both hands, she pulled his shirt apart, the pearl snaps opening in a long line. The hair was dark over his chest, arrowing down toward his jeans, and she let herself play, tweaking his nipples, tracing the curves of his abdominal muscles, bending to place little kisses wherever she could reach. His chest rose in almost a spasm whenever she touched him. Teasing him, she played with the zipper of his jeans, tight over his erection, then tugged it down slowly, only to leave it alone to reach into his pockets for a leisurely search.

With a groan, he dropped back on the floor. When she found what she'd been looking for, together they tugged at his jeans. He arched his hips, and she saw the sleek way his muscles connected to prominent bones, then disappeared beneath his dark boxer briefs. She slid her fingers along his erection slowly, up and down, and they both watched what she did. She took a long time teasing him, still straddling his thighs, her skirt cascading all around them.

"Amanda." He said her name in a hoarse, desperate whisper.

She smiled. "Now?"

He gave a weak laugh. "Please now."

She slid off his thighs and was amazed at how quickly he removed the last of his clothes. She didn't take the dress off. There was something about playing a character, being someone else that appealed to her tonight. She pushed him back on the floor and just looked at his nakedness, admiring every curve of muscle and the arousal that made her feel so wanted. She put the condom on him herself, enjoying the silky, hot hardness of him.

And then she straddled his hips and lowered herself over him, gasping with pleasure when he filled her. Breathing hard, she sank until they were hip to hip, accepting his length.

"Are you okay?" he asked.

The fact that he could think about her when a guy was normally focused on pleasure—well, that only made her feel even more special and important. And then she started to move, and it was as if they were born to work in sync. The pleasure suffused her again as his hands cupped her breasts and played with her. She leaned down to kiss him again, over and over, braced her arms on the floor and rode him, letting the sight of his nakedness arouse her as much as his hands caressing her flesh. Together they let passion rise up and consume them, until they moved faster, their bodies slick and heated. She reached orgasm again, letting it shudder over her, and as if he'd waited for her, he let go, grinding their hips together. She collapsed across his chest, breathing hard, her head pillowed against his neck. His arms folded around her, and it was heaven to be held within his embrace.

"That was . . ." He trailed off.

"I hope it was amazing, because it certainly was for me."

His chuckle rumbled deep in his chest. "Damn, there aren't words."

"Okay, I'll accept that," she said, kissing his salty skin.

The windows now held only gray light, the sun giving up for the day. At last she slid to the side, and he pulled her up against him.

"Oh, you're still wearing the dress," he said, his voice bemused.

It was now slung around her waist in an untidy mess. "So I am. And I still have to wear it Sunday, so maybe I better take it off."

"I'm not stopping you."

She sat up and pulled the dress up and over her head, then enjoyed his look of reverence as he watched her breasts. She was never going to be skinny, but apparently he didn't mind.

And then his gaze lifted to hers, and his expression sobered. "I know you'd wanted to take things slower than this."

"I did, but apparently I'm not that good at controlling myself."

His growing smile was relieved. "Because I never meant to make you feel uncomfortable."

"You didn't. I wanted this as much as you. We were playing characters, and it made me feel sexy and silly, and I haven't felt like that in forever. Maybe I needed it."

"Or maybe it was how good we are together," he said softly.

They studied each other for a long time, smiles fading.

"I don't know, Mason."

"I don't either, Amanda, but maybe the point is that we have some kind of chemistry that's rare and good. Can't we take our time and explore it?"

"But—"

"Slowly. We have all the time in the world."

Though she'd been naked and not felt shy, now she did. "Okay."

"Good. And I'm happy you're going to the rodeo tomorrow. I want to show you some of my world, introduce you to my sisters."

"Your sisters?"

"Don't sound so surprised. They brought our stock for the rodeo."

"Oh, right." Damn, that was forgetful of her.

He caressed her cheek and down around her chin, murmuring, "They'll like you a lot, I know it."

How could his sisters, related to a man like Mason, not be just as wonderful?

"Since you have to work," he said, "just call when you're ready, and I'll come get you."

"But you have to compete. I can get there alone."

"I know you can, but I want to be with you. I want everyone to see that the prettiest girl at the rodeo is with me."

His words made her feel warm and tender and flustered. And it was wonderful. "I've never been to a rodeo. What should I wear?"

"Jeans or a skirt or shorts—and cowboy boots."

She laughed. "I think I can manage that. Oh, but what time do you want breakfast?"

"Is seven too early? I'm fine with cereal or whatever's easiest."

"Cereal? After the way I worked you tonight? I think not. We'll give you a hearty breakfast: eggs, bacon, and toast. And don't protest again. In fact, I'm kinda hungry now. Shall we go search my kitchen for some snacks?"

The spent an hour in the semidarkness of her kitchen, enjoying ice cream and each other. Amanda felt like their conversation was natural and easy, like she would never run out of things to say.

Tomorrow would take care of itself.

Chapter 8

THOUGH MASON SLEPT in his own room, he dreamed of Amanda, her lush body, her uninhibitedness, her unselfishness in bed—and everywhere. He'd never met anyone like her. She'd been betrayed by a man, yet she'd been willing to give herself to Mason. She'd started her life over again, when many people might have given up, or at least settled for whatever wouldn't hurt them. He admired her, he desired her—could he fall in love with her? So quickly? Once he would have scoffed at "love at first sight," but he'd been drawn to her from the moment he'd heard her voice, let alone seen her. And though she'd wanted to take things slowly with him, she'd been unable to control the passion they inspired in each other.

As he showered and dressed, he thought about her and mused how he'd have to wait until weekends to date her—and wasn't sure he could go days between. He really had it bad.

Eager as a boy, he entered her dining room, knowing the Sassafras Girls would probably sleep in, which would mean he'd have Amanda all to himself. He inhaled the scent of bacon appreciatively, and then she came through the swinging door from the kitchen.

Her smile made something bright bloom within his soul. He opened up his arms, and she came into them easily. His concern that she'd regret their evening together faded into dust. Just the press of her body along his felt right.

He kissed the top of her head. "Good morning. Sorry to get you up so early."

"You forget you're talking to a working girl—oh wait, that sounded like I really do work at a brothel."

He chuckled.

"There's plenty of delicious food to fill you up. Now sit down and start eating. You need your energy to ride a bull!" She winced. "I'm already nervous for you."

He waved her concern away. "I'm an old pro."

"But your shoulder—"

"Will be fine. So stop worrying. I'll still be able to warm your bed tonight."

She laughed and swung her hips as she went back into the kitchen. He sat down at the table and opened the *Valentine Gazette*. Below the fold, he saw the headline "Five-Year Anniversary of Washington Sexual Harassment Scandal—Are Women Any Safer in the Workplace?"

His smile died. He started reading, and when he saw Amanda's legal name, Lauren Amanda Cramer, he groaned aloud.

"What is it?" Amanda asked with interest as she brought a hot plate in her mittened hand and set it before him. "The *Gazette* doesn't usually inspire that much emotion."

He held up the paper. "I assume you didn't read this."

"No time."

"I think you'd better."

Frowning, she took the paper from his hands, and when she saw the headline, her face paled. "Oh no," she breathed.

He waited, saying nothing. She wouldn't want to be humored or reassured. She sank into the chair next to him, and a few minutes later, she finished reading and let the paper sag as she stared at him. Though she was still pale, her eyes were dry, her expression sober.

"I was contacted about this article," she said wearily. "I wouldn't comment. I've made it a policy not to talk about it, not to relive it. It's not all about me, you know, but the slow pace of women's safety in the workplace."

"But you're featured because of the anniversary?"

She nodded. "Did you read it?"

He shook his head. "You came in just as I started, and I thought it was more important for you to see it."

She sighed. "Thanks. It would have been okay, but they even included my picture as I testified before the ethics panel. I know most people in Valentine Valley didn't remember me from the scandal. Now . . ."

"Now you'll be conspicuous." He knew this was a setback she hadn't imagined. "I'd understand if you want to stay home today, maybe wait until the memory of the article dies down a little."

She stiffened. "No. I'm not doing that anymore. I said I'm going to the rodeo, and I'm going."

Relief and admiration surged into his chest. "Amanda," he began gently.

"I'm going, and that's all there is to it. People will forget the article in a day or two, and I can go back to just being a regular person—an anonymous, regular person."

When the phone rang, she straightened her shoulders. "No one else would call this early but reporters. I'll let it go to voice mail. Now, you need to eat before your eggs get cold." She kissed his cheek as she walked past him and headed back to the kitchen.

"Call me when you're free so I can pick you up," he told her.

She simply waved and kept going. He almost felt like a jerk for putting her on display at the rodeo, where she'd be vulnerable. He wanted to protect her but didn't know if he should—or even could.

AFTER A COUPLE of hours, Amanda had to mute the sound of the ringing house phone. Luckily, her cell remained blessedly silent, except for the music filtering softly through her earbuds to distract her. She cleaned and straightened the guest suites until, at last, everything was prepped for the day and she had no other excuse for not calling Mason.

Oh, she had to get dressed. But even that only took fifteen minutes. At last she called him, and though he sounded totally casual about picking her up in twenty, she thought she heard relief in his voice.

He was her new boyfriend, and *relief* was what she inspired. It made her blink back tears of frustration. She'd vowed not to live like this anymore, letting fear control her behavior and her emotions. *She* was in charge of herself.

She was waiting on the front porch, eyes closed in meditation, when she heard the sound of an approaching truck. She opened her eyes as Mason pulled his pickup into the parking space and jumped out. Wearing a smile, she rose and went to the stairs to meet him.

When he came to an abrupt stop and gave a low whistle at the sight of her, she held her arms wide.

"You like?" she asked, feeling sexy in a short flowery pink sundress with spaghetti straps. Her cross-body purse was yellow, and her cowboy boots were carved with flowering vines.

"Wow," he breathed, striding toward her.

He lifted her off the stairs by her waist, bringing their bodies together as she slid slowly to the ground against him. The intimate touch made her breathless, and his possessive kiss brought on the good kind of dizziness.

"Let's go," she said, taking his hand and heading with determination for the truck.

"In a hurry?" He grinned as he opened the door for her.

"I'm looking forward to seeing you conquer a bull."

He grimaced.

"You're not nervous, are you?" It was her turn to tease.

"I'm just hoping I can show off for you."

Before he could shut the door, she stopped him, saying softly, earnestly, "I'll be cheering the loudest."

It wasn't a long drive to the Silver Creek Ranch, only

a mile south of Valentine Valley. But the wait was long to get into a dirt parking lot, even though Mason had a competitor parking pass.

The ranch unfolded in the shadow of the Elk Mountains, the log house, barn, and outbuildings topped with matching red roofs. Colorful tents sheltered food stands and the work of craftsmen. Mason kept up a running commentary about the ranch, how their cattle were gone for the summer at their grazing allotment in the White River National Forest, just like his were. Amanda knew he was trying to distract her, and she appreciated the effort.

Near the competition arenas, a haze of dust seemed to shimmer in the sunlight. A man with a deep Western drawl spoke over a loudspeaker, announcing events. The smell of fair food was intoxicating: sausages and onions, fried dough.

"My sisters are excited to meet you," Mason said. "Mind if we head for the stock pens?"

Holding hands, they walked the length of the parking field. Strangers smiled and nodded as they passed—and then the double takes began, the recognition in people's eyes, the whispers as they passed. She tried not to stiffen, but she noticed that Mason squeezed her hand a bit tighter.

Damn that newspaper article. Damn the five-year anniversary. Damn the senator who'd thought he could control her, bend her to his will.

And he was still controlling her after all these years, wasn't he? She wasn't going to stand for it! She wanted to be herself again, the confident woman who didn't inspire worry in her boyfriend. Already Mason meant so much to her. She didn't want to disappoint him—or herself. She smiled up at him, glad when the concern faded from his eyes.

"I guess I don't understand why you enter a rodeo," she said. "Isn't it dangerous?"

"Well, sure it is, but the life of a cowboy can be dangerous anyway, and the things we train for in the rodeo are things we sometimes do in our everyday life. Take team roping, where partners take turns roping a steer by his horns and then his hind legs until he's on the ground. We have to do that to immobilize a steer for vet treatment. And of course the rodeo life is exciting. When you're young, you want to travel around, you want to compete and show off your skills. Every day is different, and you never know what kind of bull or bronc you'll be riding. It's like the high of gambling. I loved being outside, being with animals, traveling around, meeting all kinds of people, and, in the end, testing myself. And I was good at it, until the injury. My family needing me was more important than anything else."

Mason lifted his arm and waved to someone. Amanda craned her neck and saw two young women with the same dark hair and olive complexion he had, both standing beside the corral gate. These two women were part of the family he'd sacrificed so much for.

Suddenly two teenage girls stopped right in front of Mason and Amanda, forcing them to come up short. Amanda had rehearsed this scenario over and over. She would be polite, answer questions briefly, then move on. It was just two teenage girls, wearing ponytails, a brunette and a strawberry blond.

But they weren't looking at her. Their worshipful gazes were on Mason.

"You're Mason Lopez, right?" said the blond girl breathlessly.

Her friend giggled.

Mason gave them a friendly smile. "Yep, that's me."

"We're so excited you're going to ride again!" said the blond. "I was at your last competition with my dad—I can't believe I'm lucky enough to see your return."

"My temporary return," he corrected. "I'm not going back on tour."

The two girls frowned at each other, shrugged, then held out rodeo programs. "Can we have your autograph?"

Amanda watched in disbelief and confusion as he bent his dark head to sign their rodeo programs. They looked at his autograph like it was made of gold, then backed away as they left, as if they needed to keep him in their line of sight as long as possible.

"Sorry," Mason said, taking her hand again. "I hadn't thought this would happen. I've been off the circuit for a long time."

She didn't know what to say, how to answer. Though she attracted a few sympathetic and curious stares from some older people, which she attributed to the *Gazette* article, it was nothing compared to the worship Mason's mere presence inspired in the young women gathered for the rodeo. And the dislike when those same young women saw Mason holding her hand. It gave her a chill, reminding her of the senator's supporters, who'd glared at her as if she'd deliberately engineered her boss's scandal and downfall.

He was studying her with concern. "I guess I should have told you. Maybe——"

"Mason Lopez!"

A woman in her late twenties actually shrieked his name, and Amanda gave a start. He pulled Amanda away until they reached his sisters.

The two women eyed her with friendly interest, and Amanda was glad to focus on an outthrust hand.

"Hi, I'm Sabrina," one sister said, shaking vigorously. "You must be Amanda. This is my sister Zoe. Our baby brother did nothing but talk about you this morning."

Sabrina wore her hair in a loose knot at the top of her head, while Zoe wore a low ponytail, the better for the cowboy hats in their hands. Amanda saw the resemblance to their brother in their high cheekbones and dark eyes. Sabrina was tall, with a more muscular build, whereas Zoe was petite and almost delicate. But her handshake was firm.

Amanda smiled. "It's so good to meet you both. I hope he didn't bore you."

"Not at all," Zoe said, eyeing her. "And he never even told us details, until we read them in the paper today."

Mason gave his sisters a warning frown, but Amanda waved it off. "Yeah, I didn't know the story would be published today. Guess I shouldn't have been surprised, with the anniversary this week and all."

"Bet you weren't happy to see it brought up again," Sabrina said with sympathy. "I imagine you'd rather it stayed in your past."

Amanda was touched by her understanding. "It's been difficult to live down. But I know it's an important subject, and sadly, bosses everywhere continue to take advantage."

"You must have been very brave to talk about it in front of the whole world," Zoe said, "and it's obvious you still are."

"Thanks." Amanda cleared her tight throat, knowing she was blushing.

Sabrina punched her brother lightly on the arm. "And it can't help that this big guy has women practically jumping him. I thought it'd go away by now, but no."

"It's not that bad—" Mason began.

"Not that bad?" Zoe interrupted, rolling her eyes. "We call them buckle bunnies, Amanda. Have you heard that term?"

"No," Amanda said softly.

"Every rodeo we go to, every Western town, it's the same. They want his autograph, they want his attention."

"They want to have his babies," Sabrina added. "They meet us at the stock pens in excited groups. They think Zoe and I are the enemy, like we're dating him or something."

The two women laughed together, but Mason was eyeing Amanda with renewed concern and embarrassment. "Can you two go talk to the rodeo organizer?" he asked his sisters. "I don't think we have the afternoon schedule yet."

Zoe looked confused and reached for the clipboard hung near the gate. "But I thought—"

Sabrina took her elbow and pulled. "Sure thing, Mason. We'll be back later. Nice to meet you, Amanda!"

Amanda leaned her forearms on the gate and looked into the pen, where dozens of steer grazed leisurely, unaware they were about to be wrestled to the ground. She felt a little dazed, as if she'd been doing some wrestling.

Mason stood next to her and braced his own forearms so that their elbows touched. "You okay with all of this, Amanda? I'd really thought five years away would be long enough to be forgotten, but I guess not."

In a low voice, she said, "For the whole morning, I'd told myself that today I'd get stared at and asked questions, but eventually it would die down. I just had to get through today. It was kind of my mantra, you know?"

He nodded, still watching her with his dark, somber gaze.

"But this—" She gestured toward the pen, the barns, and then him. "This is a different kind of fame, one that obviously doesn't go away."

And if she was with him, people would be staring at her, too, and not with sympathy but with envy and disappointment. Maybe there'd be crowds of people always wanting a piece of Mason, never leaving them alone, resenting her interference. She'd just found him, had thought about seeing where their relationship took them, and now . . .

She gave a laugh that held no amusement. "And to think I'd gone on and on about you not having any idea of the pressure of fame. I feel like an idiot."

"Don't," he said. "I'm the one who's an idiot. I knew what you'd faced these last few years, how brave you'd been to go public with something that wasn't your fault."

"Brave?" Now she really did sound bitter. "I've been keeping to my house! How can you call me brave?"

"Because you *are*," he insisted. "You stood up for yourself and for women everywhere. All I did was ride a bull. You've taken steps to overcome your problem. Where you've tried to put your fame behind you, to get on with your life, I made a big plan to use my fame to get noticed by an investor today." He sighed, and his broad shoulders seemed to slump. "I feel like a fake next to you."

"A fake?" She stared at him in surprise. "You're not a fake for being recognized for your accomplishments. You worked hard for them—I think Nate Thalberg would be smart to make Lake Ridge part of his investment strategy."

He turned and took her upper arms in his hands. "Would you want to be a part of whatever I accomplish, Amanda? Could you see yourself with me, even if it means being in the spotlight sometimes?"

She opened her mouth, but didn't know what to say. She thought she'd been so prepared for how the day would go—she'd reminded herself that she didn't have to answer reporters, that she could ignore whatever happened.

But wasn't that what she'd been doing for years? And what had it gotten her but imprisoned in her own home?

"Mason, I—"

"Mason!"

They both turned at the sound of Sabrina's voice.

"It's time to ride! Didn't you hear your name being called over the loudspeaker?"

Mason looked back down at Amanda with urgency. "This discussion is more important than any old ride—*you're* more important to me, Amanda."

He would give up the whole reason he'd entered the rodeo, his plan to help his family ranch—just to hear what she had to say? "Mason, you're here for your family. Please go. We can talk afterward. I'm not running away, not this time."

She met him stare for stare, wanting him to understand that she meant it. "In just a couple of days, you've become important to me, too, Mason," she said softly. "I don't want you to blow this chance. Just go. I'll be there to cheer you on."

Chapter 9

Amanda sat between Sabrina and Zoe in the stands overlooking the main arena. They chatted across her, discussing the cowboys competing against Mason and who had the best score so far. Amanda strained her eyes to watch Mason in the chute as the Lopez sisters explained things to her. They talked about how important balance was, how he had to slip his gloved hand into the bull rope and set his spurs just right.

The massive bull shifted restlessly, then the gate swung open, and Mason and the bull were flying onto the dirt arena. He had to ride for eight seconds without being bucked off, and she'd never imagined eight seconds could be so long. His entire body gyrated with the animal, who angrily tried to heave the human off his back. Mason clung to the bull with his thighs and stirrups and one arm, while the other arm flailed for balance. It was almost graceful, the way he reacted to each jump and twist of the animal.

And then a horn sounded marking eight seconds, and

she gasped as Mason flung himself to the side, rolling in the dirt as a rodeo clown jumped forward to distract the bull. Suddenly the cheers sounded loud in her ears, as if all the sound had been turned back on now that Mason was safe. Sabrina and Zoe were reaching across her to hold hands as they jumped up and down.

"Oh, he's going to get a great score for that!" screamed Sabrina over the noise of the spectators.

"I think he's going to win!" Zoe agreed.

Amanda was happy he had a chance to win, but she realized how utterly and completely relieved she was that he'd escaped injury. He was standing by the gate, grinning, talking in a relaxed fashion with another cowboy, as if he hadn't just risked his life on a wild, one-ton animal.

She was shaking with the aftermath of her relief, startled to realize how much she already cared about him. And caring about him meant being in the spotlight with him.

And suddenly, being with him was more important than anything else. The spotlight was temporary; a day-to-day life together was permanent. Did she want to try for that with Mason Lopez?

And then he looked up in the stands, and she knew in her soul he was looking for her. She jumped to her feet and waved with both arms high overhead.

He doffed his hat and waved it back at her. They were making a spectacle of themselves, and she didn't really care. Her grin must have been absolutely goofy, and the sudden tears in her eyes meant she couldn't quite focus on him.

"Do you see who he's talking to?" Sabrina said to her sister.

"That's Nate Thalberg!" Zoe answered. "They're grinning and shaking hands. Damn, this is a good sign. We'll have an investor for that champion bull yet!"

"Cowboys and cowgirls," boomed a woman's voice over the loudspeaker.

"Is it on?" said another woman, her accent strong, her voice so loud that the speaker gave a shrill squawk.

Mrs. Palmer. And that meant the first voice was Mrs. Thalberg. "Those are the widows!" Amanda said in disbelief.

"The 'Widows' Boardinghouse' widows?" Sabrina asked.

"The same."

"Heck, we've even heard of them up our way," Zoe said, shaking her head.

"Do keep speaking, Rosemary," boomed Mrs. Ludlow imperiously. "Everyone is listening."

Laughter rippled through the crowd.

"We'd like to announce," said Mrs. Thalberg, her voice full of warmth, "that we have a local celebrity in our midst!"

Amanda was thrilled for Mason. She waved at him again, ready for him to take a bow. Maybe they were going to proclaim him the bull-riding champ.

"If you read the *Valentine Gazette* today," Mrs. Thalberg continued, "then you read all about Lauren Amanda Cramer, who owns Connections B&B."

A wave of disbelief shocked her. She almost sat down, stunned, but Sabrina and Zoe linked their arms through hers, wearing proud grins.

"Five years ago, Amanda—that's what she goes by—

stood up against all of Washington, D.C., on behalf of women everywhere. We're glad she's chosen to live with us in Valentine Valley. Let's show her our appreciation!"

Mason jumped up onto the first level of the stands, and he was the first to begin to clap. Everyone else joined in, looking around for her, until all those gazes honed in on her, the sounds of the clapping a swell of thunder, all those eyes full of speculation.

And pride. She couldn't miss the pride and even admiration. So although she could swear she heard her heart pounding in her ears, she waved. Mason was coming toward her, trying to make his way up the crowded stairs. People reached to shake his hand, girls tried to touch his arms, his back, but he avoided them all. He was coming for her.

The crowd pressed all around, watching him, making her the center of attention again as he reached her, but she didn't care. He caught her in a quick, hard hug, his body warm from exertion in the July heat.

Then he held her upper arms so he could look into her face. "You okay?"

She nodded a bit like a bobble-headed doll, but she was grinning, too. He was so tall and handsome, yet so focused on her. "Yeah, yeah, I'm okay."

"I swear I didn't know they were going to announce you like that."

"I know. It's okay. *I'm* okay. Really."

Then she put her hands on his face and kissed him, to a roar of delight from the crowd.

"Well, get her out of here," Sabrina said, giving them both a push.

Grinning, Mason led her up the aisle to the top of the stands, and they escaped down the much-less-crowded rear stairs. She had to hustle to keep up with him, until he led her beneath the widespread branches of a nearby cottonwood tree. A black-and-white herding dog was lying in the shade, and although he raised his head, he calmly put it back down as if he didn't mind sharing.

And then Amanda was in Mason's arms, kissing his face, over and over. "I was so nervous. But you did so well! Your sisters think you'll win! And we saw you talking to Nate."

He laughed. "I don't know if I'll win, because there's another rider or two left. But I had a good talk with Nate, and we're going to meet up later for dinner. That's winning in my book."

"I'm so glad."

"But that's nothing compared to you getting called out in front of the crowd."

She gave a shrug and almost giggled. "It was strange, I know. But . . . I did okay. I just concentrated on my breathing and remembered that it was temporary, that I'd soon be alone with you."

He linked his hands behind her lower back, and she put hers around his neck.

"You make me feel good, Mason Lopez. You make me remember I'm strong."

"You've always been strong," he said softly, then leaned down to kiss her.

She felt light-headed looking up at him, all full of warmth and desire. "I don't know if you'll think I'm crazy, but I could fall in love with you. You've been so patient, so kind, so encouraging—"

He grimaced. "I sound like your favorite teacher, not your lover."

She laughed. "Those are all good things for a lover to be."

He kissed the tip of her nose. "I don't just *think* I could fall in love with you, Amanda Cramer. I'm mostly already there."

Their smiles died, and she stared deeply into his eyes, so dark, but shining with warmth and compassion. Their tender kiss brimmed with promise.

"Where do we go from here?" she breathed at last, feeling giddy at this newfound relationship she hadn't even imagined a few days ago.

He cleared his throat, though his voice still sounded deep and husky. "Anywhere we want. And I think I want to see you every moment I can. I'm only a half hour away."

"Might be a longer trip in the winter," she teased.

"True. It'll only be weekends at first, though I'm sure my sisters will help out."

"I'll take whatever of you I can get. I can visit you, too. I'd love to see your ranch."

"And I want to show it to you. Maybe you'd like it so much, you might think of it as home someday."

Now she felt shy, looking up at him from beneath her eyelashes. "That sounds wonderful."

And then he was holding her close, and she fit perfectly into the contours of his body. She'd come to Valentine to escape her past, and instead, she'd found her future.

This Fall . . .
Return to Valentine Valley,
where Christmas lights are twinkling
and first love burns brighter the
second time around . . .

Sleigh Bells in Valentine Valley

When Tony De Luca's ex, Kate Fenelli, waltzes through the door of his tavern and pulls up a bar stool, she turns his balanced world on end. Once they'd been each other's first love, first everything. But then life happened, and they walked away with broken hearts. Now Kate is back in Valentine, and they can't seem to stay out of each other's way. When Tony begins wondering what would happen if they rekindled the sparks, he knows he's in big trouble.

Kate can't believe she's sitting at Tony's bar spilling her life-changing problems to him. He's as gorgeous as ever, and she can't seem to forget how incredible he always made her feel. Still, the door on that chapter of their lives closed long ago. Yet with Christmas buzzing in the air, Kate can't help wondering if anything is possible—even a second chance with the only man she's ever loved.

Keep reading for a sneak peek!

Chapter 1

VALENTINE VALLEY, COLORADO, was decorated for Christmas, twinkling lights lining nineteenth-century brick or clapboard buildings, wreaths hung on shop doors, greenery wrapped around every old-fashioned lamppost. The sight used to fill Kate Fenelli with happiness whenever she came home for the holidays. But now, as she drove down Main Street the day before Thanksgiving, the decorations only reminded her of her big Italian family and how she was going to break the news to them. Humiliation and anger crawled inside her like snakes, but once again she forced them down. She had to stay in control, and she'd been reminding herself of that all through the nearly two-hour drive from Vail. She'd soon be seeing her thirteen-year-old son, Ethan. Her embarrassment would only confuse and worry him.

But the closer she got to her parents' house, the more dread built up inside her, making it difficult to swallow past the constriction in her throat. She found herself taking a turn she hadn't meant to, the Range Rover sliding a bit on the snow. Like a coward, she was circling back, away from her family, trying to find the words that would reveal enough to satisfy them but not so much that her standing with her law firm would be jeopardized.

And then she saw Tony's Tavern, a squat, plain building close to Highway 82, neon signs blinking in the windows. Three pickup trucks were parked outside, but then it was only late afternoon. She felt drawn to it by a compulsion she didn't want to acknowledge. Deliberately keeping her mind blank, she got out of her Range Rover and walked up to the door with determined steps, packed snow crunching under her boots, her breath a mist in front of her. She opened the door, and the warm air surged out at her, smelling of beer and French fries. SportsCenter was on several flat screen TVs between mounted animal heads. Two middle-aged men, looking remarkably alike in matching Carhartt jackets and cowboy hats, turned their heads the same way to glance at her. And then they each did a double take. She might have overdressed a bit today in her "I'm a professional lawyer" double-breasted wool coat and leather boots, trying to give herself confidence when she faced her family.

And then the bartender looked up at her. Tony De Luca, owner of the tavern. Her ex-husband. His brown hair always looked like it needed to be trimmed, and there was a hint of lines fanning out from the corners of his brown eyes, but then he was thirty-three, like she was. Yet . . . thirty-three looked good on him. He wore a black buttoned-down shirt, probably over jeans, although she couldn't see behind the bar. His shoulders were as broad as ever on his tall, lanky body. He'd always been an athlete, and she had a sudden memory of playing the trombone in the marching band and meeting his laughing eyes when he took off his football helmet after a big win. Back then there'd been a spark of happiness and desire and endless possibilities.

From childhood, they'd been attached, knowing what each other had been thinking, sharing the same emotions, the same bond. Tony had never been one to hide his feelings or play it cool. But all that was gone—had been gone through the nine years since their divorce. Even the sad ache of regret and bewilderment she used to feel had faded into the past. Now he was just her son's father, and since he was great at that, he had her gratitude. He had Ethan through the school week, when he could be more of a full-time parent, and she had Ethan most vacations and every weekend, when Tony always had to work. She thought it gave Ethan full-time parents for the whole week.

By the lowering of Tony's brows, Kate could tell that her appearance was unexpected; it wasn't the weekend. She'd totally forgotten that she'd told Tony last week that she was just going to stay in Vail and prepare for an important court date over the holiday.

She gave a halfhearted smile as she approached the end of the bar. "Hi, Tony."

He nodded. "Kate."

His deep voice had once made her shiver all over; now all she heard was the wariness, and it made her even sadder on this sad day.

He put down the glass he was polishing and approached her, lowering his voice as he said, "What're you doing here?"

"Can't a girl want a drink?"

His frown intensified. He poured her a glass of the house red and slid it in front of her. "If you changed your mind and decided to come for Thanksgiving, shouldn't you have rushed right to your parents' to bake pies or something?"

She grimaced. He knew she didn't bake—hell, she didn't like to cook much either, which was a sin in her family. Her parents owned Carmina's Cucina, the Italian restaurant on Main Street. She'd grown up in the business. Having served at the restaurant through her teenage years, she'd always sworn she would never be a waitress again. Why Tony had wanted the tavern, she could never understand.

She took a sip of her wine. "Tastes good."

He put both hands on the polished wood of the bar and leaned closer. "Kate, what's going on?" he demanded.

To her horror, a tear slid down her cheek, and she quickly brushed it away.

Tony's brown eyes, always the mirror of his emotions—but no longer where she was concerned—went wide. "Is something wrong? Is it Ethan?"

"No, nothing like that. I didn't mean to scare you." And then she had to wipe away another tear. "I've screwed everything up, Tony. I—I couldn't face them all at home. Not yet." She gestured bitterly to the wineglass. "Guess I needed a drink to find my courage."

"You always had courage, Kate, maybe too much of it."

She winced. Of course Tony wouldn't want to hear her complaints—he was convinced it was her fault their marriage fell apart. Oh, she shared the blame, but certainly not all of it. She should leave. She had no right to dump her problems on Tony.

"My firm put me on two months' sabbatical," she blurted out.

He crossed his arms over his chest, still frowning. But he was watching her with those deep brown eyes, the ones that had once shown her the sympathy and understanding that had made her confide everything in him.

She rushed on. "I shouldn't tell you all the details—I'm not supposed to tell anyone. I certainly won't tell my family or Ethan. But it was wrong, Tony," she insisted earnestly, her voice a hoarse whisper. "I mean, what the partners are doing is wrong, and no one will listen to me! I discovered a report my client hadn't meant to include in some papers, a report that affects their filing with the FDA—hell, it could affect the public health. In this report, people exposed to a cattle growth hormone in the research phase were having severe flu-like symptoms. But there was no proof that *that* hormone was the one my client was presenting to the FDA. I wanted more information—I thought we have a duty to the public to ask for more info, you know? But since we're not certain it specifically relates to our case, they told me to forget about it."

"And you don't take orders easily."

"Tony, that's not true. Well, not where work is concerned, anyway. So . . . I kept bringing it up to the partners, and they finally told me I could scare away this big client—or others. I never considered breaking attorney-client privilege. I could lose my license for that! But the partners don't care. They said I need to take some time and get my priorities straight, when I was just doing my job!"

Kate took a sip of wine, her hand shaky. The two men farther down the bar—who had to be twins—were making no secret of their interest. She'd kept her voice down, but now she prickled with heated embarrassment. At last she snuck another glance at Tony. His eyes were downcast, and he absently wiped a smudge on the bar. She felt a bit deflated by his attitude, but the lump had eased in her throat, at least.

She sighed. "There's nothing you can do, I know that. I'm sorry to have unburdened myself like that. You probably wish I'd leave."

It was his turn to sigh. "No, I don't. I'm a bartender; people talk to me all the time. It makes them feel better."

She winced. "You think that's the only reason I spilled my guts?"

He met her gaze, and for a moment, everything seemed to still until it was just the two of them, looking at each other across a distance of years. Had she been looking for the comfort only Tony had once given her, the security, the reassurance? There hadn't been another man like him in her life—she'd never allowed it. There had been dates and the occasional couple-month relationships, but that was it. The pain she'd felt when their marriage had crumbled . . . she'd sworn she never wanted to feel that again.

Yet here she was, telling Tony everything, like he could

make things better, just because once upon a time he'd made every bad situation look golden. But they weren't married anymore, and it looked like the casual friendship they'd shown for Ethan's sake must have been more of an illusion than she'd thought. Like she needed to be more depressed. . . .

He cleared his throat. "So what's next? How will this affect Ethan?"

She sighed. "I'll try not to let it affect him at all. I'll tell him I'm on sabbatical, but I can't tell him the confidential details I just . . . spilled to you."

"So you'll be here for Thanksgiving?"

"I guess so. Is that okay?"

His hesitation was almost invisible. Almost.

"Of course it's okay. It'll be strange for Ethan to have us both on a holiday. Just so you know, I've been invited to your mom's for dinner tomorrow."

She winced. "It's been a while since I missed a holiday; I'd forgotten that little tradition. When I'm not home for a big day, it's like you take my place with my family."

He leaned toward her, and his glance was suddenly solemn. "You know I could never do that. And if you'd rather I stay away—"

"Of course not!" she interrupted earnestly. "My family adores you."

Maybe more than they adore me, she thought with a twinge of regret.

"What about after Thanksgiving?" he asked.

"After?" she repeated, bemused.

"What do you plan to do on your . . . vacation?"

She snorted, then coughed to try to cover it. The two men down the bar grinned at her, and she gave them an awkward smile.

"*Vacation.* That's not a word I associate with this," she said through gritted teeth. "I'm being punished."

"So what are you doing for your punishment? Staying here or going back to Vail?"

Vail had once seemed a punishment to her; now it was home. She'd been made junior partner a couple years ago and been asked to open a branch of the law firm there. She'd felt like she was being thrown out of the big city of Denver, but it had been an interesting challenge. And it made seeing Ethan so much easier. But go back there, where people might ask questions when they saw workaholic Kate just hanging around? No.

"I—I don't know where I'll go," she finally admitted. "I hadn't thought that far. I just . . . couldn't stay in Vail for Thanksgiving after . . . everything that's happened. And all that trial prep I had to do? Pfft. I don't even know how I'll explain things to my family, let alone my friends."

"Or—what's his name, Keith?"

She blinked at him, watching as he picked up a glass and started polishing with deliberation. "Keith? I had a few dates with him. How did you know?"

"We do share a talkative kid."

"Oh, right." She waved a hand. "We dated. It never went further." But inside, she felt a little disturbed. Had Ethan volunteered that information—or had Tony asked him about it? She didn't know which was worse.

And suddenly, she felt more vulnerable than she had in

a long time, she, who'd always prided herself on being in control. She wasn't in control of much of anything these days.

"I guess I should go," she said, sliding her wallet out of her purse.

He frowned and put his hand on hers. "Put that away. You own a piece of this bar, remember? I'll never forget it."

She stared into those serious eyes. "Tony, it doesn't bother you, does it? You know I wanted to help."

"And I'm grateful," he said shortly.

She'd fronted the loan for him to buy the tavern a few years back—not that he'd asked, and not that he'd accepted easily. But then she'd reminded him that he'd supported her in college, helping her make her dream career come true, and she wanted to do the same for him. Tony never missed a payment to her, and he'd insisted on interest.

She hoped bringing up the loan didn't add a new layer of awkwardness to their already strained friendship—if you could call it that. She'd always wanted it to *be* a friendship, didn't want to be one of those couples who couldn't see past their anger or see what it was doing to their families. That had never been Tony and her.

But friendship? She looked at his closed-off, polite expression and suddenly knew she was kidding herself. They'd broken each other's hearts and would never recover from that. And the ache she thought she'd long ago buried suddenly made it hard to breathe.

One of the guys at the other end of the bar signaled for Tony, and he glanced at Kate.

"Go do your job," she said, forcing her voice to sound

mild rather than strained with unshed tears. "Thanks for listening."

He nodded. "See you tomorrow."

She walked out of the tavern, straightened her shoulders, and prepared to face her family.

TONY CLOSED THE cash drawer, letting his stiff back loosen when he heard the front door close. He glanced over his shoulder to see that Kate was really gone, and he felt a sense of relief, as well as a sadness so old he could blow dust off it. An older man and woman had entered in her place, wearing the more expensive coats and boots that you'd usually see up in Aspen rather than in his tavern, at least this early in the season. But even the rich liked the occasional low-key night. He saw that Rhonda, his daytime server and a mom in her forties, was gathering menus as she watched them take a seat at a table.

What the hell had Kate been thinking, coming here? He remembered his flash of surprise when she'd walked through the door, and then the momentary appreciation of her beauty, the same beauty that had been kicking him in the gut since he was a kid. She'd cut her blond hair short, and though it had been windblown when she'd walked in, he guessed she could make it look professional and neat when she wanted to. But it was her eyes that always lured him in, their purple color that was indescribable, lavender or amethyst or—thank God he wasn't still the lovesick boy who'd once composed mind-poems about her eyes. But today they'd been full of an anguish he hadn't seen in years. She could still move him to worry, and he'd had to work hard to appear disinterested. And it had hurt her, he knew, not that he took any pleasure in it, although once he might have. It was simply self-preservation.

Ned and Ted Ferguson, identical twin plumbers, glanced at each other with smirks, then back at him. They were always a day behind shaving, and their whiskers were as shot through with gray as their hair was.

"Wasn't that your ex?" Ned asked.

You could tell it was Ned, because he'd once cut his chin on a pipe, leaving a scar.

"Yep," Tony answered. "Another beer?"

Ted glanced down at his half-full bottle and eyed his brother. "He doesn't want to talk about her."

Tony sighed. "There's nothing to talk about. She's home for Thanksgiving. Our kid'll be happy."

"But not you?" Ned prodded.

"Guys—"

"I don't like to see my ex," Ned continued as if Tony hadn't spoken. "And she don't look anywhere near as good as yours. Yours has done good for herself."

"Classy," Ted added, the twin who always agreed more than instigated. "But then, Ned, your ex could give a horse a run for its money."

Tony sighed and walked away. The twins bantered but never took offense, and as Ned shot back a good-natured retort, Tony found himself staring unseeing at SportsCenter on the closest TV.

Kate had certainly been flustered, but she'd never met a situation she couldn't conquer. She had a fierce will to succeed. It had attracted him to her, but it had also been one of the causes of their breakup. They'd been in the same class in kindergarten, but she'd just been another girl then. It wasn't until fourth grade, when she'd developed a friendship with his sister, Lyndsay, a year younger than them, that Tony had come into contact with Kate outside school. He'd found himself playing the role of annoying older brother for a while. Only in hindsight had he realized he'd been trying to get Kate's attention even then. She'd been like the sun shining on his world, vibrant and happy and so driven—always so driven, he thought, shaking his head. She'd wanted to be the smartest student, the best trombone player, the fastest cyclist, and being around her and all that energy had been exciting. He hadn't even minded that she liked to be in charge all the time.

By high school they were a couple. He accepted his sister's teasing, Kate's brothers' protectiveness—none of it mattered. The future seemed far away; he lived for his moments with her, kissing her, touching her. He even got a part-time job bussing tables at her parents' restaurant so they wouldn't have to be separated. During the summer, he hung around at the end of each day at the local law firm where she interned, hoping to buy her ice cream or walk her home. And when Cal Carpenter, one of the lawyers, said she could always work for him after she graduated, Tony started deceiving himself about their future.

Together they went off to college in Denver, though she'd landed a full ride at the best university. He played down how much he loved her, how she was the center of his world. He knew that scared her, and he was willing to let her go for her dreams, never wanting to stand in her way.

And then she got pregnant the summer after their freshman year, and everything between them changed. She was panicky and scared, but he wasn't. He'd always meant to marry her, to be a family. The thought of their baby just thrilled him. They were young, but they'd have all the time in the world to be parents, unlike his mom, who died before she was even fifty.

But their marriage only lasted four years—four years during which the pressure of college and jobs and a baby stressed their little family. It didn't break it, though, until the final realization that he and Kate didn't want the same kind of future together after all.

"You look like crap."

Tony looked up to see Will Sweet taking the seat Kate had just vacated. Will was a tall cowboy with sandy hair, hazel eyes, and a cleft in his chin that set the girls' eyelashes fluttering. Of course his devil-may-care attitude and constant flirting helped.

"Nice to see you, too," Tony said dryly.

Will parked his cowboy hat on the stool beside him and eyed Tony. "Was that Kate Fenelli I just saw looking as grim as death as she drove off in that fancy Range Rover?"

Tony nodded. Without being asked, he poured a draft beer and set it in front of his friend. "She's got some time off, so don't be surprised to see her around."

"You okay with that?"

Tony's eyes widened. "Why wouldn't I be? This is her hometown, same as mine. And Ethan'll be glad."

Will snorted before taking a sip of beer and smacking his lips. "Good stuff. Yeah, the kid's always happy to see his mom, which says good things about her, I guess."

Tony grinned. "That compliment was dragged out with reluctance."

Will shrugged. "She's always been gorgeous, but I never thought she was your type."

"I have a type?" Tony countered, glad to be feeling amused again.

"She might have been born here, but she's a city girl at heart, and you're, well, you're practically a rancher, you're so small town."

"*You're* the rancher—I'm just a simple barkeep. And she lives in Vail now, remember."

"But I bet she misses Denver. To think she tried to force you to live there. Like you or Ethan would have been happy."

Tony kept his smile in place, although it was strangely difficult. "That's old news, Will. And it wasn't just her wanting to live in Denver, and me here, that ruined our marriage."

Will harrumphed, even as he took another sip of beer. "Then what was it? You don't exactly talk about it much."

Tony hesitated, then spoke softly. "It's hard to talk about the biggest failure of your life."

Will eyed him, then looked around. "I'd like to listen."

Tony chuckled. "It's my job to listen." There weren't many people he'd unloaded his problems on, and he wasn't going to start now. "Thanks, but it's in the past. I've moved on."

"Really, with who?"

"Hey, I've dated."

"I can't think of anyone who lasted longer than three months. I think you're way too loyal to a memory."

"I haven't met the right girl. And I have Ethan, you know. I have to be careful. I really don't intend to marry again until he's an adult. Why traumatize him that way?"

Will's only response was a snort.

But inside, Tony was worried that he'd met the *only* girl for him and, since their relationship was ruined, he'd never have another. Their breakup had shattered him. She'd seen the real person inside him—and hadn't wanted him.

More and more lately, he was reminding himself how good his life was, with family, friends, and the best son in the world. More and more he was trying to prove to himself that everything was as it was meant to be.

But he was trying too hard.

A Guide to Emma Cane's
Valentine Valley

"Strong families, deep friendships and
sexy heroes abound in Valentine Valley.
I'd love to live there."

#1 *New York Times* bestselling author Sherryl Woods

A Town Called Valentine

A Valentine Valley Novel, Book 1

Emily Murphy never thought she'd return to her mom's rustic hometown in the Colorado Mountains. But after her marriage in San Francisco falls apart, leaving her penniless and heartsick, she returns to her old family home to find a new direction for her life. On her first night back, though, a steamy encounter with handsome rancher Nate Thalberg is not the fresh start she had in mind . . .

Nate has good reason not to trust the determined beauty who just waltzed into town; he's no stranger to betrayal. Besides, she's only there to sell her family's old property and move back out. But as Nate and Emily begin working side by side to restore her timeworn building, and old family secrets change Emily's perception of herself, both are about to learn how difficult it is to hide from love in a place known far and wide for romance, family ties, and happily-ever-afters: a town called Valentine.

True Love at Silver Creek Ranch

A Valentine Valley Novel, Book 2

Adam Desantis is back—bruised, battle-weary, and sexier than ever! Not that Brooke Thalberg is in the market. The beautiful cowgirl of Silver Creek Ranch needs a cowboy for hire, not a boyfriend—though the gaggle of grandmas at the Widows' Boardinghouse thinks otherwise. But from the moment she finds herself in Adam's arms, she's shocked to discover she may just want more.

Adam knows it's crazy to tangle with Brooke, especially with the memories that still haunt him and the warm welcome her family has given him. But he finds himself in a fix, because tender-loving Brooke is so much more woman than he ever imagined. Can a soldier battling demons give her the love she clearly deserves?

Just about everybody in Valentine thinks so!

A Wedding in Valentine

A Valentine Valley Novella

Bridesmaid Heather Armstrong arrives for Nate and Emily's big weekend, only to discover that one of the ushers is the man she had a close encounter with when they were trapped by a blizzard seven months before—and he's the bride's brother!

Cowboy Chris Sweet never forgot the sexy redhead, although she'd disappeared without a trace. At first the secret creates a divide between them, but as they grow closer during the romantic weekend, will Heather dare risk her heart again?

"The Christmas Cabin"

from the anthology
All I Want for Christmas Is a Cowboy

*It's Christmas in Valentine, and the Thalbergs remember
how their family came to be. . .*

Sandy, recently diagnosed with MS and abandoned
by her husband, is determined to make Christmas special for her three-year-old Nate. While they're trooping
through the woods to cut down their Christmas tree, a
snowstorm arises, and a mysterious old ranch hand points
them toward an abandoned cabin. Little do they realize
that the ranch hand also guides cowboy Doug Thalberg to
the same place . . .

The Cowboy of Valentine Valley

A Valentine Valley Novel, Book 3

Ever since a heated late-night kiss—that absolutely should not have happened—cowboy Josh Thalberg makes former Hollywood bad girl Whitney Winslow's pulse beat faster. But when she decides to use his gorgeous leatherwork in her new upscale lingerie shop, Leather and Lace, she's determined to keep their relationship strictly professional . . . even if she wants so much more.

Josh has never met a challenge he isn't up for. Which is probably why he allowed Whitney to persuade him to take the sexy publicity photo that went viral—and now has every woman in America knocking down his door . . . every woman except for the one he can't get out of his head.

But how to convince a reformed bad girl that some rules are worth breaking?

A Promise at Bluebell Hill

A Valentine Valley Novel, Book 4

From the moment Secret Service agent Travis Beaumont strides into town and through the door of Monica Shaw's flower shop, she feels a sizzle of attraction. After years of putting everyone else's needs first, Monica is ready to grab hold of life. If she can just persuade the ultimate protector to let his own walls down for once . . .

The president's son is getting married in Valentine Valley, and Travis should be avoiding all distractions . . . not fantasizing about a forthright, sexy-as-hell florist. Especially when she's keeping secrets that could jeopardize his assignment. But just this once, Travis is tempted to put down the rulebook and follow his heart—right to Monica's door.

Roses are red, violets are blue, and in Valentine Valley, love will always find you.

EMMA CANE grew up reading and soon discovered that she liked to write passionate stories of teenagers in space. Her love of "passionate stories" has never gone away, although today she concentrates on the heartwarming characters of Valentine, her fictional small town in the Colorado Rockies.

Now that her three children are grown, Emma loves spending time crocheting and singing (although not necessarily at the same time), and hiking and snowshoeing alongside her husband, Jim, and two rambunctious dogs, Apollo and Uma.

Give in to your impulses . . .
Read on for a sneak peek at eight brand-new
e-book original tales of romance
from Avon Books.
Available now wherever e-books are sold.

THE COWBOY AND THE ANGEL
By T. J. Kline

FINDING MISS McFARLAND
THE WALLFLOWER WEDDING SERIES
By Vivienne Lorret

TAKE THE KEY AND LOCK HER UP
By Lena Diaz

DYLAN'S REDEMPTION
BOOK THREE: THE McBRIDES
By Jennifer Ryan

SINFUL REWARDS 1
A BILLIONAIRES AND BIKERS NOVELLA
By Cynthia Sax

WHATEVER IT TAKES
A TRUST NO ONE NOVEL
By Dixie Lee Brown

HARD TO HOLD ON TO
A HARD INK NOVELLA
By Laura Kaye

KISS ME, CAPTAIN
A FRENCH KISS NOVEL
By Gwen Jones

An Excerpt from

THE COWBOY AND THE ANGEL

by T. J. Kline

From author T. J. Kline comes the stunning
follow-up to *Rodeo Queen*. Reporter
Angela McCallister needs the scoop of her
career in order to save her father from the bad
decisions that have depleted their savings. When
the opportunity to spend a week at the
Findley Brothers ranch arises, she sees a chance
to get a behind-the-scenes scoop on rodeo.
That certainly doesn't include kissing the
devastatingly handsome and charming cowboy
Derek Chandler,
who insists on calling her "Angel."

"Angela, call on line three."

"Can't you just handle it, Joe? I don't have time for this B.S." It was probably just another stupid mom calling, hoping Angela would feature her daughter's viral video in some feel-good news story. When was she ever going to get her break and find some hard-hitting news?

"They asked for you."

Angela sighed. Maybe if she left them listening to that horrible elevator music long enough, they'd hang up. Joe edged closer to her desk.

"Just pick up the damn phone and see what they want."

"Fine." She glared at him as she punched the button. The look she gave him belied the sweet tone of her voice. "Angela McCallister, how can I help you?"

Joe leaned against her cubical wall, listening to her part of the conversation. She waved at him irritably. It wasn't always easy when your boss was your oldest friend, and ex-boyfriend. He quirked a brow at her.

Go away, she mouthed.

"Are you really looking for new stories?"

She assumed the male voice on the line was talking about the calls the station ran at the ends of several news programs asking for stories of interest. Most of them wound up in her mental "ignore" file, but once in a while she'd found one worth pursuing.

"We're always looking for events and stories of interest to our local viewers." She rolled her eyes, reciting the words Joe had taught her early on in her career as a reporter. She was tired of pretending any of this sucking up was getting her anywhere. Viewers only saw her as a pretty face.

"I have a lead that might interest you." She didn't answer, waiting for the caller to elaborate. "There's a rodeo coming to town, and they are full of animal cruelty and abuse."

This didn't sound like a feel-good piece. The caller had her attention now. "Do you have proof?"

The voice gave a bitter laugh, sounding vaguely familiar. "Have you ever seen a rodeo? Electric prods, cinches wrapped around genitals, sharp objects placed under saddles to get horses to buck . . . it's all there."

She listened as the caller detailed several incidents at nearby rodeos where animals had to be euthanized due to injuries. Angela arched a brow, taking notes as the man gave her several websites she could research that backed the accusations.

"Can I contact you for more information?" She heard him hemming. "You don't have to give me your name. Maybe just a phone number or an email address where I can reach you?" The caller gave her both. "Do you mind if I ask one more question—why me?"

"Because you seem like you care about animal rights.

That story you did about the stray kittens and the way you found them a home, it really showed who you were inside."

Angela barely remembered the story other than that Joe had forced it on her when she'd asked for one about a local politician sleeping with his secretary, reminding her that viewers saw her as their small-town sweetheart. She'd found herself reporting about a litter of stray kittens, smiling at the animal shelter as families adopted their favorites, and Jennifer Michaels had broken the infidelity story and was now anchoring at a station in Los Angeles. She was tired of this innocent, girl-next-door act.

"I'll see what I can do," she promised, deciding how to best pitch this story to Joe and whether it would be worth it at all.

An Excerpt from

FINDING MISS McFARLAND
The Wallflower Wedding Series
by Vivienne Lorret

Delany McFarland is on the hunt for a
husband—preferably one who needs her
embarrassingly large dowry more than a dutiful
wife. Griffin Croft hasn't been able to get Miss
McFarland out of his mind, but now that she's
determined to hand over her fortune to a rake,
Griffin knows he must step in. Yet when his
noble intentions flee in a moment of unexpected
passion, his true course becomes clear: tame
Delaney's wild heart and save her from a fate
worse than death . . . a life without love.

SHE *HAD* BEEN purposely avoiding him.

Griffin clasped his hands behind his back and began to pace around her in a circle. "Do you have spies informing you on my whereabouts at all times, or only for social gatherings?"

Miss McFarland watched his movements for a moment, but then she pursed those pink lips and smoothed the front of her cream gown. "I do what I must to avoid being seen at the same function with you. Until recently, I imagined we shared this unspoken agreement."

"Rumormongers rarely remember innocent bystanders."

She scoffed. "How nice for you."

"Yes, and until recently, I was under the impression that I came and went of my own accord. That my decisions were mine alone. Instead, I learn that every choice I make falls under your scrutiny." He was more agitated than angered. Not to mention intrigued and unaccountably aroused by her admission. During a season packed full of social engagements, she must require daily reports of his activities. Which begged the question, how often did she think of him? "Shall I quiz you on how I take my tea? Or if my valet prefers to tie my cravat into a barrel knot or horse collar?"

"I do not know, nor do I care, how you take your tea, Mr. Croft," she said, and he clenched his teeth to keep from asking her to say it once more. "However, since I am something of an expert on fashion, I'd say that the elegant fall of the mail coach knot you're wearing this evening suits the structure of your face. The sapphire pin could make one imagine that your eyes are blue—"

"But you know differently."

Her cheeks went pink before she drew in a breath and settled her hand over her middle. Before he could stop the thought, he wondered whether she was experiencing the *fluttering* his sister had mentioned.

"You are determined to be disagreeable. I have made my attempts at civility, but now I am quite through with you. If you'll excuse me . . ." She started forward to leave.

He blocked her path, unable to forget what he'd heard when he first arrived. "I cannot let you go without a dire warning for your own benefit."

"If this is in regard to what you overheard—when you were eavesdropping on a *private matter*—I won't hear it."

He doubted she would listen to him if he meant to warn her about a great hole in the earth directly in her path either, but his conscience demanded he speak the words nonetheless. "Montwood is a desperate man, and you have put yourself in his power."

Her eyes flashed. "*That* is where you are wrong. I am the one with the fortune, ergo the one with the power."

How little she knew of men. "And what of your reputation?"

Her laugh did nothing to amuse him. "What I have left

of my reputation will remain unscathed. He is not interested in my person. He only needs my fortune. In addition, as a second son, he does not require an heir; therefore, our living apart should not cause a problem with his family. And should he need *companionship*, he is free to find it elsewhere, so long as he's discreet."

"You sell yourself so easily, believing your worth is nothing more than your father's account ledger," he growled, his temper getting the better of him. He'd never lost control of it before, but for some reason this tested his limits. If *he* could see she was more than a sum of wealth, then *she* should damn well put a higher value on herself. "If you were my sister, I'd lock you in a convent for the rest of your days."

Miss McFarland stepped forward and pressed the tip of her manicured finger in between the buttons of his waistcoat. "I am *not* your sister, Mr. Croft. And thank the heavens for that gift, too. I can barely stand to be in the same room with you. You make it impossible to breathe, let alone think. Neither my lungs nor my stomach recalls how to function. Not only that, but you cause this terrible crackling sensation beneath my skin, and it feels like I'm about to catch fire." Her lips parted, and her small bosom rose and fell with each breath. "I do believe I loathe you to the very core of your being, Mr. Croft."

Somewhere between the first *Mis-ter-Croft* and the last, he'd lost all sense.

Because in the very next moment, he gripped her shoulders, hauled her against him, and crushed his mouth to hers.

An Excerpt from

TAKE THE KEY AND LOCK HER UP

by Lena Diaz

As a trained assassin for EXIT Inc—a top-secret
mercenary group—Devlin "Devil" Buchanan
isn't afraid to take justice into his own hands.
But with EXIT Inc closing in and several
women's lives on the line, Detective Emily
O'Malley and Devlin must work together to find
the missing women and clear both their names
before time runs out . . .
and their key to freedom is thrown away.

"I WANT TO talk to you about what you do at EXIT."

"No."

She blinked. "No?" Her cell phone beeped. She grabbed it impatiently and took the call. A few seconds later she shoved the phone back in her pocket. "Tuck's outside. The SWAT team is set up and ready to cover us in case those two yokels decide to start shooting again. The area is secure. Let's go." She headed toward the door.

"Wait."

She turned, her brows raised in question.

He braced his legs in a wide stance and crossed his arms. "If I'm not under arrest, there's no reason for me to go to the police station."

Her mouth firmed into a tight line. "You're not under arrest only if you agree to the deal I offered. The man who killed Shannon Garrett and the unidentified victims in that basement is holding at least two other women right now, doing God only knows what to them. All I'm asking is that you answer some questions to help me find them, so I can save their lives. Doesn't that mean anything to you?"

Of course it did. But he also knew Kelly Parker, and anyone with her, couldn't be saved by Emily and her fellow cops. It was becoming increasingly clear that Kelly was the bait in a trap to catch *him*. The killer would keep her alive, maybe even provide proof of life at some point, to lure Devlin to wherever she was being held. Did he care about her suffering? Absolutely. Which meant he had to come up with a plan to save her without charging full steam ahead and getting himself killed. Because once the killer eliminated his main prey—Devlin—he'd have no reason to keep either of the women alive.

He braced himself for his next lie. If Emily thought he was bad to supposedly get a woman pregnant and abandon her, she was going to despise him after this next one.

"Finding and saving those women is your job," he said. "I have other things to do that are a lot more fun than sitting in an interrogation room."

The shocked, disgusted look that crossed her face was no worse than the way he felt inside. Like a jerk, and a damn coward. But if sacrificing his pride kept her safe, so be it. He had to get outside and offer himself as bait to lead his enemies away from the diner before she went out the front. He strode past her to the bathroom door.

"Stop, Devlin, or I'll shoot."

He slowly turned around. Seeing his sexy little detective pointing a gun at him again seemed every kind of wrong, especially when his blood was still raging from the hot kiss they'd just shared.

"Seriously?" he said, faking shock. "You're drawing on an unarmed man? *Again*? What will Drier say about that? Or Alex? I smell a lawsuit."

She stomped her foot in frustration.

The urge to laugh at her childish action had him clenching his teeth. She was the perfect blend of innocence, naiveté, and just plain stubbornness. Before he did something they'd both regret—like kissing her again—he slipped out of the bathroom.

A quick side trip through the kitchen too quickly for anyone to even question his presence, and he was down the back hallway, standing at the rear exit. Now all he had to do was make it to some kind of cover—without getting shot—and lead Cougar and his handler away from Emily, all without a weapon of his own to return fire.

Simple. No problem. He shook his head and cursed his decision to go to the police station this morning. Then again, if he hadn't, he wouldn't have gotten to kiss Emily. If he were killed in the next few minutes, at least he'd die with that intoxicating memory still lingering on his lips.

He cracked the door open and scanned the nearby buildings. Then he flung the door wide and took off running.

An Excerpt from

DYLAN'S REDEMPTION
Book Three: The McBrides
by Jennifer Ryan

From *New York Times* bestselling author
Jennifer Ryan, the McBrides of Fallbrook
return with Dylan McBride, the new sheriff.
Jessie Thompson had one hell of a week.
Dylan McBride, the boy she loved, skipped
town without a word. Then her drunk of a
father tried to kill her, and she fled Fallbrook,
vowing never to return. Eight years later,
her father is dead, and Jessie reluctantly goes
home—only to come face-to-face with the
man who shattered her heart. A man who,
for nearly a decade, believed she was dead.

STANDING OVER HER sleeping brother, she held the pitcher in one hand and the cup of coffee in the other. She poured the cold water over her brother's face and chest. He sat bolt upright and yelled, "What the hell!"

Brian held a hand to his dripping head and one to his stomach. He probably had a splitting headache to go with his rotten gut. As far as Jessie was concerned, he deserved both.

"Good morning, brother. Nice of you to rise and shine."

Brian wiped a hand over his wet face and turned to sit on the sodden couch. His blurry eyes found Jessie standing over him. His mouth dropped open, and his eyes went round before he gained his voice.

"You're dead. I've hit that bottom people talk about. I'm dreaming, hallucinating after a night of drinking. It can't be you. You're gone and it's all my fault." He covered his face with his hands. Tears filled his voice, his pain and sorrow sharp and piercing. She refused to let it get to her, despite her guilt for making him believe she'd died. Brian needed a good ass-kicking, not a sympathetic ear.

"You're going to wish I died when I get through with you, you miserable drunk. What the hell happened to you?" She handed over the mug of coffee and shoved it up to his mouth to make him take a sip. Reality setting in, he needed the coffee and a shower before he'd concentrate and focus on her and what she had in store for him.

"Don't yell, my head is killing me." He pressed the heel of his hand to his eye, probably hoping his brain wouldn't explode.

Jessie sat on the coffee table in front of her brother, between his knees, and leaned forward with her elbows braced on her thighs.

"Listen to me, brother dear. It's past time you cleaned up your act. Starting today, you are going to quit drinking yourself into a stupor. You're going to take care of your wife and child. You're going to show up for work on Monday morning clear eyed and ready to earn an honest day's pay."

"Work? I don't have any job lined up for Monday."

"Yes, you do. I gave Marilee the information. You report to James on Monday at the new housing development going up on the outskirts of town. You'll earn a decent paycheck and have medical benefits for your family.

"The old man left you the house. I'll go over tomorrow after the funeral to see what needs to be done to make it livable for you and Marilee. I, big brother, am going to make you be the man you used to be, because I can't stand to see you turn into the next Buddy Thompson. You got that?" She'd yelled it at him to get his attention and to reinforce the fact that he'd created his condition. His eyes rolled back in his head, and he groaned in pain, all the reward she needed.

"If you don't show up for work on Monday, I'm coming after you. And I'll keep coming until you get it through that thick head of yours: you are not him. You're better than that. So get your ass up, take a shower, mow the lawn, kiss your wife, tell her you love her and you aren't going to be this asshole you've turned into anymore. You hear me?"

"Your voice is ringing in my head." He stared into his coffee cup, but glanced up to say, "You look good. Life's apparently turned out all right for you."

Jessie shrugged that off, focused more on the lost look in Brian's round, sad eyes.

"I thought you died that night. I left and he killed you. Where have you been?"

"Around. Mostly Solomon. I have a house about twenty miles outside of Fallbrook."

"You do?" The surprise lit his face.

"I started my life over. It's time you did the same."

An Excerpt from

SINFUL REWARDS 1
A Billionaires and Bikers Novella
by Cynthia Sax

Belinda "Bee" Carter is a good girl; at least,
that's what she tells herself. And a good girl
deserves a nice guy—just like the gorgeous
and moody billionaire Nicolas Rainer. Or
so she thinks, until she takes a look through
her telescope and sees a naked, tattooed man
on the balcony across the courtyard. He has
been watching her, and that makes him all
the more enticing. But when a mysterious
and anonymous text message dares her to
do something bad, she must decide if she is
really the good girl she has always claimed
to be, or if she's willing to risk everything
for her secret fantasy of being watched.

An Avon Red Novella

I'D TOLD CYNDI I'd never use it, that it was an instrument purchased by perverts to spy on their neighbors. She'd laughed and called me a prude, not knowing that I was one of those perverts, that I secretly yearned to watch and be watched, to care and be cared for.

If I'm cautious, and I'm always cautious, she'll never realize I used her telescope this morning. I swing the tube toward the bench and adjust the knob, bringing the mysterious object into focus.

It's a phone. Nicolas's phone. I bounce on the balls of my feet. This is a sign, another declaration from fate that we belong together. I'll return Nicolas's much-needed device to him. As a thank you, he'll invite me to dinner. We'll talk. He'll realize how perfect I am for him, fall in love with me, marry me.

Cyndi will find a fiancé also—everyone loves her—and we'll have a double wedding, as sisters of the heart often do. It'll be the first wedding my family has had in generations.

Everyone will watch us as we walk down the aisle. I'll wear a strapless white Vera Wang mermaid gown with organza and lace details, crystal and pearl embroidery accents, the bodice fitted, and the skirt hemmed for my shorter height. My hair will be swept up. My shoes—

Voices murmur outside the condo's door, the sound piercing my delightful daydream. I swing the telescope upward, not wanting to be caught using it. The snippets of conversation drift away.

I don't relax. If the telescope isn't positioned in the same way as it was last night, Cyndi will realize I've been using it. She'll tease me about being a fellow pervert, sharing the story, embellished for dramatic effect, with her stern, serious dad—or, worse, with Angel, that snobby friend of hers.

I'll die. It'll be worse than being the butt of jokes in high school because that ridicule was about my clothes and this will center on the part of my soul I've always kept hidden. It'll also be the truth, and I won't be able to deny it. I am a pervert.

I have to return the telescope to its original position. This is the only acceptable solution. I tap the metal tube.

Last night, my man-crazy roommate was giggling over the new guy in three-eleven north. The previous occupant was a gray-haired, bowtie-wearing tax auditor, his luxurious accommodations supplied by Nicolas. The most exciting thing he ever did was drink his tea on the balcony.

According to Cyndi, the new occupant is a delicious piece of man candy—tattooed, buff, and head-to-toe lickable. He was completing armcurls outside, and she enthusiastically counted his reps, oohing and aahing over his bulging biceps, calling to me to take a look.

I resisted that temptation, focusing on making macaroni and cheese for the two of us, the recipe snagged from the diner my mom works in. After we scarfed down dinner, Cyndi licking her plate clean, she left for the club and hasn't returned.

Three-eleven north is the mirror condo to ours. I straighten the telescope. That position looks about right, but then, the imitation UGGs I bought in my second year of college looked about right also. The first time I wore the boots in the rain, the sheepskin fell apart, leaving me barefoot in Economics 201.

Unwilling to risk Cyndi's friendship on "about right," I gaze through the eyepiece. The view consists of rippling golden planes, almost like . . .

Tanned skin pulled over defined abs.

I blink. It can't be. I take another look. A perfect pearl of perspiration clings to a puckered scar. The drop elongates more and more, stretching, snapping. It trickles downward, navigating the swells and valleys of a man's honed torso.

No. I straighten. This is wrong. I shouldn't watch our sexy neighbor as he stands on his balcony. If anyone catches me . . .

Parts 1 and 2 available now!

An Excerpt from

WHATEVER IT TAKES
A Trust No One Novel
by Dixie Lee Brown

Assassin Alex Morgan will do anything to save
an innocent life—especially if it means rescuing
a child from a hell like the one she endured. But
going undercover as husband and wife, with
none other than the disarmingly sexy Detective
Nate Sanders, may be a little more togetherness
than she can handle. Nate's willing to face
anything if it means protecting Alex. She may
have been on her own once, but Nate has one
more mission: to stay by her side—forever.

WHAT WAS ALEX doing in that bar? She had to be following him. It was too much of a coincidence any other way. Nate nearly flinched when he replayed the image of her dropping Daniels and then turning on those goons getting ready to shoot up the bar. Shit! Was she suicidal along with everything else? Anger, tinged with dread, did a slow burn under his collar. He needed to know what motivated Alex Morgan . . . and he needed to know now.

He clenched his teeth, whipped his bike into an alley, and cut the engine. If she was bent on getting herself killed, there was no fucking way it was happening on his turf.

She dismounted, uncertainty in her expression. As soon as she stepped out of the way, he swung his leg over and got in her face. "Take it off." He pointed to the helmet.

Not waiting for her to remove it all the way, he started in. "What in the name of all that's holy were you thinking back there? You could have gotten yourself killed."

A sad smile swept her face and something in her eyes—a momentary hardening—gave him a clue to the answer he was fairly certain she'd never speak aloud. Ty had told him the highlights of her story. Joe had freed

Alex from a life of slavery in a dark, dismal hole in Hong Kong. From the haunted look in her eyes, however, Nate would bet she hadn't completely dealt with the aftermath. His first impression had been more right than he wanted to admit. It was quite likely that she nursed a dangerous little death wish, and that's what had prompted her actions at the bar.

His anger receded, and a wave of protectiveness rolled over him, but he was powerless to take away the pain staring back at him. He could make a stab at shielding her from the world, but how could he stop the hell that raged inside this woman? Why did she matter so much to him? Hell, logic flew out the window a long time ago. He didn't know why—only that she *did*. With frustration driving him, he stepped closer, pushing her against the bike. Her moist lips drew his gaze, and an overwhelming desire to kiss her set fire to his blood.

She stiffened and wariness flooded her eyes.

He should have stopped there, but another step put him in contact with her, and he was burning with need. He pulled her closer and gently slid his fingers through her hair, then stroked his thumb across her bottom lip.

Her breath escaped in uneven gasps and a tiny bit of tongue appeared, sliding quickly over the lip he'd just touched. Fear, trepidation, longing paraded across her face. Ty's warning sounded in his ears again—she was dangerous, maybe even disturbed—but even if that was true, Nate wasn't sure it made any difference to him.

"Don't be afraid." *Shit!* Immediately, he regretted his words. This woman wasn't afraid of anything. Distrustful . . .

yes. Afraid? He didn't even want to know what could scare her.

Her eyes softened and warmed, and she stepped into him, pressing her firm body against his. He caught her around the waist and aligned his hips to hers. Ignoring the words of caution in his head, he bent ever so slowly and covered her mouth with his. Softly caressing her lips and tasting her sweetness, he forgot for a moment that they stood in an alley in a questionable area of Portland, that he barely knew this woman, and that they'd just left the scene of a real-life nightmare.

He'd longed to kiss her since the first time they'd met. She'd insulted his car that day, and not even that had been enough to get his mind off her lips. Good timing or bad—kissing her and holding her in his arms was long overdue.

An Excerpt from

HARD TO HOLD ON TO
A Hard Ink Novella
by Laura Kaye

From *New York Times* and *USA Today* bestselling
author Laura Kaye comes a hot, sexy novella to
tie in with her Hard Ink series. When "Easy"
meets Jenna, he has finally found someone to
care for, and he will do anything to keep her safe.

As THE BLACK F150 truck shot through the night-darkened streets of one of Baltimore's grittiest neighborhoods, Edward Cantrell cradled the unconscious woman in his arms like she was the only thing tethering him to life. And right at this moment, she was.

Jenna Dean was bloodied and bruised after having been kidnapped by the worst sort of trash the day before, but she was still an incredibly beautiful woman. And saving her from the clutches of a known drug dealer and human trafficker was without question the most important thing he'd done in more than a year.

He should have felt happy—or at least happier—but those feelings were foreign countries for Easy. Had been for a long time.

Easy, for his initials: E.C. The nickname had been the brainchild years before of Shane McCallan, one of his Army Special Forces teammates, who now sat at the other end of the big back seat, wrapped so far around Jenna's older sister, Sara, that they might need the Jaws of Life to pull them apart. Not that Easy blamed them. When you walked through fire and somehow came out the other side in one piece, you gave thanks and held tight to the things that mattered.

Because too often, when shit got critical, the ones you loved didn't make it out the other side. And then you wished you'd given more thanks and held on harder before the fires ever started raging around you in the first place.

Easy would fucking know.

The pickup paused as a gate *whirr*ed out of the way, then the tires crunched over gravel and came to a rough stop. Easy lifted his gaze from Jenna's fire-red hair and too-pale face to find that they were home—or, at least, where he was calling home right now. Out his window, the redbrick industrial building housing Hard Ink Tattoo loomed in the darkness, punctuated here and there by the headlights of some of the Raven Riders bikers who'd helped Easy and his teammates rescue Jenna and take down the gangbangers who'd grabbed her.

Talk about strange bedfellows.

Five former Green Berets and twenty-odd members of an outlaw motorcycle club. Then again, maybe not so strange. Easy and his buddies had been drummed out of the Army under suspicious, other-than-honorable circumstances. Disgraced, dishonored, disowned. Didn't matter that his team had been seriously set up for a big fall. In the eyes of the US government and the world, the five of them weren't any better than the bikers they'd allied themselves with so that they'd have a fighting chance against the much bigger and better-armed Church gang. And, when you cut right down to it, maybe his guys weren't any better. After all, they'd gone total vigilante in their effort to clear their names, identify and take down their enemies, and clean up the collateral damage that occurred along the way.

Like Jenna.

"Easy? *Easy?* Hey, *E*?"

An Excerpt from

KISS ME, CAPTAIN
A French Kiss Novel
by Gwen Jones

In the fun and sexy follow-up to *Wanted: Wife*,
French billionaire and CEO of Mercier Shipping
Marcel Mercier puts his playboy lifestyle
on hold to handle a PR nightmare in the
US, but sparks fly when he meets the
passionate captain of his newest ship . . .

Penn's Landing Pier
Philadelphia
Independence Day, 5:32 AM

"Of course I realize he's your brother-in-law," Dani said, grinning most maliciously as she dragged the chains across the deck to the mainmast. "In fact I'm counting on it as my express delivery system." She wrapped a double length of chain around her waist. "My apologies for shamelessly exploiting you."

"Seriously?" Julie laughed. "Trust me, I'll try not to feel compromised."

"Like me," Dani said, her hair as red as the bloody blister of a sun rising over the Delaware. She yanked another length of chain around the mast. "But what can *I* do. I'm just a *woman*."

"And I'm just a media whore," Julie said. "And a bastard is a bastard is a bastard." She nodded to her cameraman, flexing her shoulders as she leveled her gaze into the lens. "How far would you go to save *your* job?"

Two days later
L'hôtel Croisette Beach
Cannes

PINEAPPLE, MARCEL MERCIER deduced, drifting awake under the noonday sun. A woman's scent was always the first thing he noticed, as in the subtle fragrance of her soap, her perfumed pulse points, the lingering vestiges of her shampoo.

Mon Dieu. How he loved women.

"Marcel," he heard, feeling a silky leg slide against his own.

He opened his eyes to his *objet d'affection* for the past three days. "*Bébé . . .*" he growled, brushing his lips across hers as she curled into him.

"Marcel, *mon amour*," she cooed, fairly beaming with joy. "*Tu m'as fait tellement heureuse.*"

"What?" he said, nuzzling her neck. Her pineapple scent was driving him insane.

She slid her hand between his legs. "I *said* you've made me very happy." Then she smiled. No—*beamed*.

He froze, mid-nibble. Oh no. Oh *no*.

She kissed him, her eyes bright. "I don't care what Paris says—I'm wearing my *grand-mère*'s Brussels lace to our wedding. You wouldn't mind, would you?"

He stared at her. Had he really gone and done what he swore he'd never do again? He really needed to lay off the absinthe cocktails. "Mirabel, I didn't mean to—"

"Why did you leave me last night?" she said, falling back against the chaise, her bare breasts heaving above the tiny triangle of her string bikini bottom. "You left so fast the maids are still scrubbing scorch marks from the carpet."

Merde. He really ought to get his *dard* registered as a lethal weapon. He affected an immediate blitheness. "I had to take a call," he said—his standard alibi—raking his gaze over her. She really was quite the babe. "I didn't want to wake you."

All at once she went to full-blown *en garde*, shoving her face into his. "*Really.* More like you couldn't wait to get away from me. And after last night? After what you asked me?" Her enormous breasts rose, fell, her gaze slicing into his. "You said . . . You. *Loved. Me.*"

Had he? *Christ.* He needed to diffuse this. So he switched gears, summoning all his powers of seduction. "Mirabel. *Chère.*" He smiled—lethally, he knew—cradling her chin as he nipped the corner of her mouth. "But that call turned into another, then three, and before you knew it . . ." He traced his finger over the bloom of her breasts and down into the sweet, sweet cavern between them, his tongue edging her lip until she shivered like an ingénue. "You know damn well there's only one way to wake a gorgeous girl like you."

"You should've come back," she said softly, a bit disarmed, though the edge still lingered in her voice. "You just should have." She barely breathed it.

"How, *bébé*?" He licked the hollow behind her ear, and when she jolted, Marcel nearly snickered in triumph. Watching women falling *for* him nearly outranked falling *into* them. "Should I have slipped under the door?" he said, feathering kisses across her jawline. "Or maybe climbed up the balcony, calling 'Juliet? Juliet?'"

She arched her neck and sighed, a deep blush staining her overripe breasts. Marcel fought a rush of disappointment. Truly, they were all so predictable. A bit of adulatory stroking and it was like they performed on cue. She pressed against his chest as he tugged the bikini string at her hip, her mouth opening in a tiny gasp.

"Mar-*cel* . . ." she purred.

He sighed inwardly. It was almost *too* easy. And that was the scary part.